Secrets Beyond the Map

Garrison Gusikowski

Contents

Chapter 1

Loria pov

I'm loria i live in abria city I'm the only one here that is 17 all the people that live in abria are married couples and they even don't get pregnant my mom was the only one here that got pregnant and for that i don't have a father.

my mom says that the city punished her by taking my father away she don't talk too much about it but when i sneak to the family album i see my father's photo everywhere here in the city he was so young in those photos he was smiling to my mom in every photo he loved her and this city took him from her, from me and for that i hate this city.

"loria wake up its 9 am we have to go"

That was my mom yelling from downstairs"I'm coming" i said. I hate this city, i hate this work and i hate this house even more

I got up went to the shower and after about 15 minutes i got out yeah i know fast shower the long shower will be when i return. i stood in front of the mirror after i dressed looking at myself i wasn't so bad i have light brown long hair that i sweared i won't ever cut it unless i got out from this city, brown eyes and a curvy body that i really hate.

"didn't you hear your mother yelling from downstairs for you!" my grandmother said entering my room. i really love grams i look alot like her except for the eyes they said i got it form father

"yeah grams i heared her and I'm on my way for her you won't come with us today?" i asked "no sweety i will rest today i feal my back acing" she said "okay". and with that i hugged her, said goodbye and went straight to my mom that will kill me for being late.

"what took you so long i was waiting for you here for half an hour" my mom said"yeah sorry mom i overslept" i apologized"well hurry up we are already late" she said "mom why are we late for our own farm. This is our farm we can be late if we want to and even if we didn't go who will get angry except your stupid story about the city that will be angry if we didn't work" i said "it's not stupid the story is true and the city's anger is so bad we can't take it i can't risk you taken from me like your dad " she said "okay mom okay let's hurry up" we reached the farm and start working.

Kai pov

"we need more money for our project the project is not over yet there are things we need to do" i said to my siblings.

"relax kai the clubs are giving us enough money and we still have so much time to show our project" my brother max said"well i actually think that we cancel this stupid project it is not worth the money we spent on it" my brother nik said "i swear this stupid brothers are gonna end me" i said in my mind.

"well nik if you want to go spend the money on your little whores I'm not gonna stop you but you will not come running to me after the project is done am i making my self clear?" i said "dude i don't want money to spent on my girls i just want you to relax you are so tense since this project starts" nik said " and i will be until the project is over so fuck off" i said they got up and get out of the office.

Let me introduce myself I'm kai lionail I'm the smart one from my brothers and I'm the one who created this project. actually we have alot of money me and my siblings but i want to do something else i want to use my intelligence i think that i got all of it while we are in our mother's womb yes the three of us are at the same age we are Tribble but we don't look alike all of us got the same brown hair and the same blue eyes but we are different for example i love sports so i have an athletic body nik loves food so he is not in the perfect shape and there is max he is mix from both of us. But this project is really good i really love it and i don't actually know why they don't give a fuck about it. There was only a one Defoe in a lot of years but i dealt with it and the project is stable again.

I got out of the office heading to my room to rest a little bit it's 12 am i have to rest my eyes a little to have a clear mind to complete the project.

I went to the room and suddenly i was attacked "happy birthday" by my mother. i literally forgot that it was my birthday " mom what are you doing! " i said "what do you mean?

I came here to celebrate with you" my mom pouted "and where is max and nik ?" i asked "they are celebrating their birthday outside with their friends" she explained "come on give your mom a hug" she continued "mom you know that I'm 24 right?" i asked "yes darling of course. what? Do you want something on your birthday?" she asked " no mom i mean that I'm old enough and stop calling my darling" i said "you will never be old to me" she said hugging me

   "boss your father wants to see you" Daniel my right hand said " okay Daniel I'm coming" i said dismissing him.

Chapter 2

Loria pov

    After a long day in the farm i finally got home it was a very long day. After i got my long shower that took an hour and a 30 minutes finally it's the best time in the day the time when i go to the roof listening to music

I'm in love with the sky i love the sky so much and i love to go to the roof putting my headphone on and just watching the clouds moving.

I was thinking about my mother's story. mom was always telling me that the city is alive and that the city was punishing those who aren't working hard enough but i didn't really believe in that but also there is that unsolved puzzle that there is no one here around my age the people that live in the city are afraid of being pregnant because they are afraid of the city afraid that what happened to my father would happen to them so they don't risk and when i was thinking i realized something there is a library here in the city so i could go to the library and search for anything in the books that will tell me anything about this city's history.

Next morning..I woke up early than i supposed to and went straight so the library

"hello i was searching about history books" i said to the librarian " it's in section c" she replied. I thanked her and went to section c searching for the history books and not any book i want a history book about the city but i found nothing all i found was the world's history and some maps and i didn't even find our city in the maps.

"can i help you with something.?" a beautiful woman said " oh thanks i was just searching about some book about the city but i didn't find anything" i said

The woman seemed surprised well it is surprising that there is nothing about the city that you live in. in any book and it's not even on the maps "maybe they are in another section" she said "maybe" i said "anyway i should go it was nice meating you" i continued and with that i ran back to my house my mom is gonna kill me if she knew i talked to a stranger.

"where were you? your mom was searching for you" grams said "i was just getting some fresh air" i said "okay okay go for her" grams said i gave her a kiss and i went searching for mom

"where the hell were you?" my mom yelled at me "i was just getting some fresh air" i said "fresh air? In 9 am?" she said "actually i woke up at 7 " i said "and where were you?" my mom asked "well i will tell you but you will not get angry at me" i pouted "where were you loria? " my mom yelled at me "okay okay i was in the library" i said "why were you in the library?" my mom asked confused "i was searching for a history book about the city" i said

My mom was confused as fuck she was just staring at me waiting for me to continue

"mom i was searching about a book about the city and guess what i found nothing there is nothing about the city in books the city is not even on maps" i said

"You don't believe me. That's why you searched in books. Just like your father" my mom said and started crying.

I was confused my mom didn't say that my father was searching about the city's history she didn't say anything like that before why would she say that now? my eyes watered at the thought of my father and i couldn't hold myself anymore

"what the fuck are you talking about! my father was taken because you got pregnant not because he was searching in books stop scaring me stop controlling me stop doing that mom i can't take it anymore" i yelled at me mother's face and i immediately regret it.

"you think I'm juat scaring you! . You think I'm lying! Your father was searching in books and he found something but he refused to tell me because i was pregnant and when i insisted we had a fight and from that day i didn't see him or hear from him he ran away i told you that the city took him because if I said that he ran away you would hate him " she said crying

And with that my world start falling apart all my life i have hated this city because it took my father but all this was a lie my father was the one that gave up on me on us he ran away without explaining to my mom one fight and he was gone but what makes her say the truth! maybe she just lied to keep controlling me.

"i don't believe you" i said "if you don't believe me go to the library and ask the librarian about the book that vulian was searching in" my mom said "i can't hold you anymore and if you don't believe me then search for what you father has found" my mom said "i will and i will get the hell out of this stupid city".

Chapter 3

K ai pov

    "Mi hai chiamato papà" i said to my father (you called for me father) "yes kai i wanted to talk to you" my father said "about!" i said "about your project" he said and i knew what he will talk to me about

  "i said nothing about your project because you are the boss i put you in this position as my heir because you are capable of dealing with it not your two stupid brothers all they want is to go to club and spend their money on alcohol and girls" my father said "yes father i know all of that but what do you want to talk to me about my project? " i interrupted

  "your project is taking to much money and time you don't sleep how are you supposed to deal with all the mafia stuff without getting any sleep?" my father asked "papà Il mio progetto è importante per me" i said (my project is important to me)

  "Lo so ed è per questo che ti sto chiedendo di terminare questo progetto così possiamo tornare alla nostra vita" my father yelled (I know and that's why I'm asking you to end this project so we can go back to our life)

"okay father i will try my best" i said clenching my jaw "you can go now" he said

I went to my office furious because of the way he talked to me with I'm the mafia boss he gave me this position. He is no longer the boss or the tough lionail he can't yell at me like this. he can't do this.

I got up went straight to the gym it's a thing i do when I'm angry but before i could enter the gym Kristina stopped me "we have a problem" she said "about what?" i asked "about your project" she said

Loria pov

I went to the library after my fight with my mom i wasn't gonna believe it of course she is lying to me why wouldn't she.! . She tried to control my life a thousand times why would she tell me the truth now? but i have to get a prove then I'm done with her

"hello how can i help you" the librarian said when i approached her "I'm actually looking for a book" i said "what book?" she asked "a book that vulian was searching in" i said "oh of course one minute" she said fake smiling.

There is actually a book so my mom wasn't lying to me about it my father really left us here he just walked away. But how? this city don't have any airports or any sea and i don't think there is a secret tunnel or something i really have to stop reading fantasy books

"here" the librarian said giving me a small book. This is the book that my father had fight with mom because of it "thank you" i thanked her, got the book and went to a table in the library to see what is the secret that my father kept.

I opened the book and i found nothing. it was a children book it was a story about the moon and some kids want to go to the moon. Is that what my father found? well i think there is something i don't see but what is it! i will have to take this book to my house.

I got home after a long day i went to the farm after the library and had another fight with my mom about the book and that i don't believe her and that was a plan she organized with the librarian to make me stop and other things that i really don't remember

I went straight to the roof it's the time that i really love in the day. I opened the book that i got with me from the library to start thinking with a clear mind but nothing. i got nothing. what did my father found out? and then i saw something weird the moon in this book is not like our moon. the city's moon's light is different

What the hell am i thinking about! it's a kids book of course it wouldn't be the real moon i have to stop my mind from thinking because it doesn't make any sense I'm really tired i probably should go get some rest.

Unknown pov

"What is the boss yelling about at his office?" i asked " we don't know Kristina is inside it's something about the project" Daniel said "what would make the boss so angry about the project like that? " i asked again "he was angey like this one time and we all know why" Daniel said smirking

"Cosa sta succedendo dentro" max said (what is happening inside) "we don't know it's something about the project" Daniel said "i think my brother lost his mind" max said entering the office

After a while

"Mio fratello ha perso la testa" max said (My brother has lost his fucking mind) "what happened to you? " niora said "your fucking boy attacked me because of his stupid project" max yelled

slap "Controllati, stai parlando con tua madre" niora said (Control yourself you are talking to your mother) "Mi dispiace mamma" max said and went straight to his room (I'm sorry mother)

Niora went straight to the boss's office and all we could hear is yelling and after a while the boss got out looking furious he looked to me and said "it's all because of you".

Chapter 4

Loria's pov

"good morning" grams said opening the windows. "good morning grams" I said "come on we are going to the farm" she said "but grams it's early" i said "yeah i know but we are going to return early as well" grams explained

I got up from the bed went to shower then dressed in a skinng jeans and an oversized hoodie.

"you look sweet baby" grams said "thanks grams" i said smiling "come on we are going to be late" my mom interrupted "mom i want to talk to you" i said "about?" my mom asked "about all the city stuff" i said

After a while we were setting in the living room "look mom I'm sorry that i didn't believe you about the city stuff but you kept those things away from me you didn't tell me that my father has left us i lived all my life thinking that the city took it from us you made me hate the city" i said "i didn't tell you because i didn't want you to hate your father" my mom said "i know and I'm sorry that i yelled and all the drama i did" i said "it's okay baby come here" my mom said hugging me "come on go to the farm and we will catch up with you" my mom said smiling

After a while in the farm

"mom I'm tired can't we just take a break" i said "no Loria we have to work hard if you want to be back early" my mom said

At night

"loria come on the dinner is ready" mom yelled i went downstairs with my father's book in my hand "why did you bring that stupid book to the table" my mom said "I don't know i have a feeling that there is something wrong" i said

"the wrong thing is that book on the table loria can you please return it to the library so we could get back to our life!" my mom said "okay mom I will return it tomorrow"

At the roof

"why do i feel that there is something wrong!" i said. wait what it that?The moon light is different than yesterday the moon light today is not the same light as yesterday how is that!

I opened the book again and found the moon light changed. Yesterday the light was different than the story and today it's the same color. How is that possible?

Oh my God that is not the moon

Kai pov

"i want to know how that happened? " i yelled at Kristina after i got inside my office again. "i don't know i told you what happened why are you yelling now" Kristina yelled back

"Daniel dice a Max che lo voglio adesso" i yelled (Daniel tell max that i want him now) "on it boss" Daniel said and went outside the office "we need to deal with this situation" I said to Kristina "we will just calm down" Kristina said

"Cosa vuoi?" max yelled opening the door (what do you want?) "Controlla il tuo fottuto tono e non dimenticare che stai parlando con il capo italiano" i yelled back (Control your fucking tone and don't forget that you are talking to the Italian boss)

"yes boss" max said "i want you to deal with some problem" i said "and may i ask what is that fucking problem?" max said "it's about the project" i said "Ovviamente è" max said (Of course it is)

"max that is not the right time just listen carefully" i said he nodded his head " i want you to be in the project" i said "what do you mean?" he asked "i mean i want you in the project. we are going to send you to abria" i said.

Chapter 5

Kai pov

"what?? Why??" max said "because there is a trouble girl in abria" i explained "Perché non ti occupi di lei?" max said (why don't you deal with her) "well I'm trying to" i yelled "Preparati, stai andando. alla fine della discussione" i continued ("Get ready, you're going to. end of the discussion)

Max ran to the door without saying a word i know he is mad but i can't send anyone but him i can't go myself because all the mafia stuff and nik is not responsible enough to send him he will probably just make things worse "Kristina i want this problem solved by tomorrow night" i said "Si Capo" Kristina said (yes boss)

And i will deal with him.

Loria pov

This is not the moon this is lighting poles "oh my God i need to tell mom and grams" i said

I hurried downstairs "mom grams hurry to the living room please there is a problem" i yelled while I'm on my way to the living room. I saw my mom coming out from the kitchen and my grand mother looking at me from the sofa she is sitting on in the living room "what is happening loria!? " grams said "i want a meeting with you two right now" i said my mom sat on the sofa next to grams looking at me confused

"i think this city is not real you guys didn't realize that there is no moon here " i started

Mom : "what you mean there is no moon and how you explain the light in the dark!?""this light is fake they use some lighting poles to provide us with this light they want us to believe that this city is real" i explained. Grams : "and why anyone would do that you have to stop reading those fantasy books" i looked at her with furious eyes i hate when people say that.

"grams I'm sure about what I'm telling you okay. last nigh the moon light was kinda yellow and the moon light in this book was different too it was white and today the moonlight in the sky is white and in the book is also white" i said opening the book infront of them "are you saying that this stupid children book is your prove that the city is not real?!" my mom yelled "mom calm down there is alot of proves that this city is not real. this city is not even on the fucking maps" i yelled "loria go to your room" grams said "what? What do you mean go to..." "i mean go to your room now" my grams interrupted me

I went to the roof again with the book in my hand there is only one way to find out the truth

The next day

I woke up to find out that I'm still on the roof with the book in my hands holding it tight this book is the key to every thing with this book i will find out what happend with my father why he left us and how he got out of this city.

I went downstairs to my room took a 15 minute shower thinking about what i will findout today i was afraid of the truth but still the truth is the truth no matter how much it takes. i grapped my momfit jeans and an oversized hoodie put my hair in a messy bun and went to the library again

"hello loria you came to give the book back i see" the librarian said "yeah of course I'm going to return the book but actually that's not what i was here for" i said " well what are you here for?" the librarian asked "I'm here to see if there is any other books like this one" i said " yeah of course you can find them in section a" she explained "and where is section a!? " i said " i can show you where it is" a handsome man said

I looked at his blue eyes and i could see that he is a stranger i have never saw him before his straight brown shoulder length hair his muscles his jaw.

"thank you for offering i was just going to tell her to ask someone to take here there because i have lots of work now" the librarian said looking at the handsome man " yeah sure" he said "ladies first" he continued i looked at him and went straight ahead of him.

" well you didn't tell me your name" he said " i wasn't going to" i said "and why is that?" he stepped infront of me "because you are a stanger and i don't like strangers and also I'm sure that your wife will not be happy about you flirting with some other girl you just met" I said"i wasn't flirting" he said smiling "or do you want me to" he continued smirking.

"you are looking at me like I'm some kind of a meal to you and I'm not interested so can you just tell me where is section a?" i said looking him in the eye he looked at me then direct his finger to a section faraway from where we stand "thanks" i said and went to where he pointed

Well there is a lot of books here but why? not like there is any children here"if you tell me what you are looking for i could help you" the man from earlier said resting his back against the corner of the section.

"i think that i made myself clear I'm not interested" i said not looking at him "but we didn't even officially met why don't you give me a chance!" he said "I'm max and you?" he said putting his hand infront of him so i can shake it. wait a minute there is no marriage ring in his fingers how is that? "I'm loria and why you are not wearing your marriage ring?" i asked "maybe because I'm not married" he said. WHAT THE HELL!!

Chapter 6

Kai pov

"boss we have a problem" Kristina said opening the office's door. "Cazzo. what is the problem now?" i said "your brother i think he just made another problem in abria" Kristina said taking a step back "HA FATTO COSA! " i said looking at her with furious eyes (HE DID WHAT!)

Loria pov

What did he just say?? He is not married?? How? all the people in this city are married i think he is just playing around.

"you are lying" i said looking at his eyes with coldness "I'm not" he said smirking "how is that possible! all people in abria are a married couples" i said "Cazzo" he said running away this city is gonna end me (fuck)

A few days later

I didn't find anything all i found was just some place that someone saw my father going to. the night of the fight. it's a trampoline i think he was coming here so he can take off the stress and maybe he came here after his fight with mom because he was just angry. i didn't tell my mom about this place because i know she will be angry and maybe she will ask someone to take the trampoline from this place to any-where so i can forget about dad. she dont like it when i talk about him in the house anymore she even don't like when i go to the roof she said that it made me insane because of the moonlight story.

"hey there" max said.

yeah me and max are spending alot of time together in the library he told me that he don't remember anything about his parents that he just found himself in this city without any-one of course i didn't tell him anything about the moonlight story and about the moonlight. it still changes everynight from white to yellow and from yellow to white

"hey max" i replied "what are you thinking about?" he asked "nothing i was just staring into the sky i love it here" i said "yeah it's a great place" he said laying next to me.

watching the sky together i introduced him to my fami-ly and they loved him so much grams said that he is not responsible for being lonely or about his parents my mom thinks that he is a stranger and that i have to stay away from him but i don't really listen to her.

"do you think we are a Defoe in this city!" i asked "what are you talking about?" he asked back "I'm saying that we are the only ones here that aren't a married couple there must be something wrong" i said still looking at the sky "well we can change that" he said looking at me smirking "ew i can't even imagine it" i said laughing "what? Why? Am i that ugly! You know that you broke my heart right!" he said pouting "you know that you are like a big brother to me max. and yes you are that ugly" i said looking at him i was totally lying he is not even that close to ugly he was handsome as fuck but he was a big brother

Kai pov

"well then bring him back here before he destroys every-thing" i yelled at arma "i can't he is now a part of her life and if we just took him she is going to be sure that there is something wrong and maybe even see the door like her father" arma said

Arma is my best freind he is clever just as me he is also my partner in this project he knows alot of things that i can't think of sometimes. When I'm angry he must be here because when I'm angry i can do some shitty things only him can fix it.

"arma I'm not losing this project i spent alot of money on it" i said "i know Kai but you have to clear your mind so you can take a decision you can't take any decision when you are that mad" he said "Come posso non essere arrabbiato, il mio stupido fratello mi ucciderà?" i yelled at his face (How can i not be mad my stupid brother is gonna end me)"Ηρέμησε" he said (calm down)"we are gonna solve this problem just like we solved the other one" he continued yeah arma is greek i met him when i was in a tour around the world he stood by my side when i was at Greece and since then he became my best friend.

Loria pov

"mom don't yell at me" i said to my mother

yes we were arguing. AGAIN. but today was because of max she didn't want me to talk to him anymore she even closed the door in his face today without telling me that he was here she don't have that right I'm going to be 18 in a week so she will not have the right to yell at me or control me anymore i even can leave the house and go to any place in this stupid city since i don't know a way out from it. YET

"i will yell at you as much as i like loria" mom said "you are my fucking daughter i will not let you do whatever you want" she continued. well i have had enough "MOM DON'T YELL AT ME" i yelled at her face "I'm not a little girl anymore I'm going to be 18 I'm going to leave this damn house i will not allow you to control me anymore" i finished *slap* yup she slapped me just like this.

"you are grounded you will not go out from your room for a whole week DO YOU UNDERSTAND ME!?" she yelled

I ran to my room holding my tears refusing to let them go i will not cry infront of her to give her satisfaction i went to the roof and closed the door behind me this place is full of shit and i will not wait for my birthday to go.

Chapter 7

Loria pov

It's midnight the whole city is asleep now i don't know where to go but i will not stay with mom anymore maybe i will go to the trampoline place built a house and live there maybe i will sleep in any inn for a couple of days i will sleep anywhere but not in this house. i went to my room grabbed my bag put my clothes in it and went to where my legs took me i wasn't thinking i was just looking at the sky and my legs are moving without me knowing to where.

I found myself in the trampoline place i jumped on it took my stress out i was jumping without thinking jumping to take my stress off. i was thinking about my mom, grams, my father, max and i was thinking about my shitty life. Until i felt myself flying to the sky

HOW THE HELL IS THAT POSSIBLE!!

Kai pov

"Capo abbiamo bisogno di te in ufficio c'è un problema sul progetto about" Daniel said entering my room quickly out of breath (Boss we need you in the office there is a problem about the project)"Quello che ha fatto mio fratello adesso?" i said coming out from the shower wearing only my boxers (What my brother did now?)

"go down Daniel i will be right there" i said going to the dressing room i picked only a sweatpants and went straight to the office i entered the office to find my men surrounding someone

"clear the road" i ordered they began to let me in and then i saw her HOW THE HELL DID SHE GOT OUT?

"Portami Arma ora" i ordered olin one of my men that was standing next to me (bring me arma now)

"well well well. what are we going to do to you now" i said to her "what the fuck do you mean? And where the hell am i?" she said "first you are in Italy second. how did you got out of abria?" i asked Leaning closer to her she didn't flinch she stared in my eyes with her brown eyes wow she has a beautiful eye "i don't know" she said not leaving eye contact "well we are gonna find out soon" i said "chiudila in cella" i ordered Daniel (Lock her in the cell) "Che cazzo vuoi dire chiudimi in una cella?" she said looking me in the eyes well that's new i didn't know she was talking Italian (What the fuck do you mean lock me in a cell?) "i mean lock you in a cell what part of it you don't understand!" i said "who are you? " she said "I'm kai lionail" i said looking at her eyes she looked confused for a second then "you are max's brother" oh hell no he didn't just tell her about us i will kill him.

i stormed out of the office hearing her calling for me asking questions like what am i doing here? Where i am? Why are you taking me to a cell? And another questions

Loria pov

What the fuck was That where am i!? what is that man talking about?! how is he max's brother?! he can't be. max has no one he has no brother no sister no mother or father he was lonely he told me that he remembered that they died in an accident. and where the hell am i! how I'm in italy? and how an i talking Italian? i didn't learn that language i didn't learn any language i just learnt Arabic because my mom taught me it how did i understood what he said! and even replied to him in his language what the hell am i?

"hey i can fucking walk on my own can you stop grabbing my shoulder and squeezing it?" i glared at the man that was taking me to the cell his name is Daniel i don't know how i know that but i know so much about him i don't know how i just met him.

"stay in here don't try to escape because you can't. so don't bother" he Said after shoving me inside a cell my head hit the wall hard it really hurts but i kept my face straight without giving any reaction he won't get a reaction from me not today not ever he got out of the cell and close it behind him and after he was gone the light gone off but I was still able to see but i wasn't seeing myself i was seeing with someone's eyes i don't know how he was out from the dungeon and went to the office where i was "she is in the cell boss" the man said "great Daniel you can go now" kai said WHAT THE HELL AM I SEEING WITH DANIEL'S EYES NOW!!!

kai pov

"arma she talked to me in fucking Italian how is that possible! the library in abria wasn't containing any dictionary to any language" i told arma "maybe Max taught her" arma said "of course no she was talking like me like she was born Italian she wasn't talking like some girl that someone taught her some words a few days ago" i said looking at the documents infront of me about her "she is his girl" i realized "she is his girl" i said again "whos?" arma asked "vulian's" i answered handing him the paper in my hand

"open the cell" i was in the dungeon going to her the man opened the door and she was right there sitting on the floor her eyes closed her head resting on the wall her brown thigh long hair is in a messy bun I'm sure she did it when she entered the cell because her hair wasn't tied when she was in my office i grabbed the water from the floor and splash her with it then crouched beside her she opened her eyes taking a shaky breath looking at me with her beautiful eyes i wipped the water from her eyes and looked at them

" we need answers and you are gonna giva it to us" i said beside me arma looking at her "well i have some too" she said looking at arma and me "well let's hear the first question" i said "why the fuck i can read your mind?" she asked SHE CAN DO WHAT?

Chapter 8

K ai pov

"what??" i asked confused as fuck what the hell that's not possible i think she reads so much fantasy books "do you think that you will lie to me and i will believe you that easy??!" i said looking in her eyes damn this girl has a beautiful brown eyes i can't stop looking at them.

"if it was a lie how would i know that you are thinking my eyes are beautiful!" she asked arma looked at me like he was waiting for an answer from me "Arma non guardarmi così e pensa come diavolo può farlo hell! " i yelled at him (Arma don't look at me like that and think how the hell she can do that!)

Arma was looking at her focused in her eyes she didn't look at him she was looking at me directly in my eyes like she was trying to focus on me" yes I'm trying to focus on you so i can get some answers to myself " she said

What? Did i said that aloud?!" no you didn't say that aloud I'm reading your fucking mind remember! "she said looking at me with bored eyes" why don't you tell me what I'm thinking about? "arma said getting closer to her she looked at him and focused for a couple of minutes.

Loria pov

What? Why the hell i can't read his mind?? Am i capable of reading max's brother 's mind only! But why! This doesn't make any sense

"i can't read your mind" i said looking at the blond guy that stands beside max' s brother i know his name is kai but i don't give a fuck.."why not?" the blonde man asked " i don't know i only can hear his thoughts" i said pointing to max's brother he was looking at me not breaking eye contact [i think she is just playing she just guessed a thing or a two relax she is not reading your mind] i heared max's brother's mind "dude I'm not playing with you I'm saying the truth i can hear your thoughts" i said looking at his eyes

And suddenly everything went black and i started seeing with someone's eyes again. i think it's Daniel again he is the only one i can do this with "uccidi questa ragazza, questo progetto deve finire qualunque cosa accada" some man said with his back to Daniel i couldn't see his face i could only see his brown hair (kill the girl. this project must end no matter what happens) "Si Capo" he replied then got out of the room (yes boss)

Kai pov

She was staring at the wall behind me we tried talking to her we pushed her she wasn't responding what is she doing?

"what happened to her?" Arma asked " i don't know I'm with you in this fucking cell" i yelled at him and her eyes came back to my face she was coughing trying to take her breath what the fuck is happening to her??

"what happened?" arma asked "nothing" she said she seemed to be thinking of something "I'm not thinking of anything" she said looking at me

Yeah i forgot mind reading "so how did you got out of abria?" arma asked "i don't know i was just jumping on some trampoline and i found myself flying to the sky how is that possible? I thought that there is gravity and that you can't do that" she replied to arma "well it is not possible that you flew to here you maybe just went to the door but how did you know where it is?" i asked "how many times am i going to tell you that i don't know!" did she just yelled at me! *slap* yes i slapped her I'm the mafia boss no one can raise his voice to me especially not some whore.

"I'm not a fucking whore" she said looking at me with blood dripping from her nose "i don't give a shit and since you are already in my mind then you must know who I'm. you can't raise your voice at me" i explained looking at her

She wasn't breaking eye contact "do i seem like i give a fuck about who you are?" she said looking at me daring me to say anything else "Voglio informazioni nel mio ufficio stasera, occupatevi di lei" i said to Daniel that entered the cell recently (I want information to my office tonight deal with her) " "   shd said raising her eyebrow (is that supposed to make me frightened?)

Of course she is talking Arabic her mother taught her this language.

"No, ma deve averti fatto riflettere due volte prima di rispondere a qualsiasi domanda" i said and headed to the cell door (No but it must made you think twice before answering any questions)

Loria pov

What the hell was that supposed to mean! He just went out of the cell after giving order to Daniel to take information out of me but i don't know anything

"well how about we start with the simple questions?" Daniel said taking his black suit jacket off "i don't know anything i answered the questions that i knew" i said "Penso che lo scopriremo" Daniel said starting hitting me (I think We will find out)

After a couple of hours

I was on the floor my nose is bleeding i think i have a broken rip or two and i have lots of bruises.

"so don't you remember anything!" he said getting ready to give me another kick to my stomach "don't you think i would have saved myself all this!" i said looking at his eyes

[Bene, penso che sia ora di farlo, ha detto il capo] i heared his thought (Well i think it's time to do what the boss said) he took his gun out fron his waist and pointed it at me

Well i think i now know who is the girl that he man with the brown hair gave the order to kill its me.

Chapter 9

Loria pov

Daniel was pointing a gun at me well i think that's how my life ends before it even starts i mean for god sake I'm 17 year old and I'm in a cell all bruised with a gun pointed at me waiting for the bullet to end my fucking life

The door went open to reveal a shocked kai "Che diavolo sta succedendo qui?" he said looking at Daniel (What the hell is happening here) Daniel removed his gun from my face and looked at kai he wasn't speaking "i said what is happening here! What are you doing? I don't remember giving you an order to kill her." kai said "boss i wasn't going to i was just frightening her So she can answer your questions" Daniel lied

"dude that's a terrible lie" i said still on the floor looking at them "Chiudi quella fottuta bocca" Daniel growled at me (Shut your fucking mouth) "why? are you afraid that I'm gonna tell him that you were ordered to kill me" i said "what??" kai said with a stone face "by who!?" kai asked looking at me "i don't know but by someone he called boss" i explained earning a kick to my stomach from Daniel.

"loca come here" kai yelled and some other guy went in he was a black man with a black hair and a wonderful green eyes what is wrong with these men all of them are fucking beautiful.

"Porta Daniel in ufficio" he ordered "si capo" the black man said (Take Daniel to the office) and they were out of the cell.

"how did you know that Daniel was ordered?" kai asked "i saw him talking to the man" i said "how? You didn't leave the cell" kai said with a confused look on his face "yeah I know but still i saw them but i didn't saw them with my eyes i saw them with Daniel's" i explained "how?" he asked i told him everything that happened that i even saw him talking with someone about one of their warehouses he was looking at my eyes searching for a reason so that he can trust me

Kai pov

She told me all about her super powers I'm still amazed I'm trying to control my mind so she won't be able to read my mind i was focusing on some memory about an enemy i killed i thought that it would make her fear me and if she was lying to stop the lies

"so you are telling me that you have a super power but you can only use it on me or Daniel" i said "yup" she said she looked so tired she was covered in bruises "well. come with me" i said standing up "where?" she asked i lookes at her without saying anything "you are not gonna tell me are you!" she said i still didn't answer

She tried to stand up but she was all bruised she couldn't stand i think that's from the broken rips i offered her my hand and she took it i never thought that she will accept my help

"well that wasn't so hard was it !" i said "what?" she asked innocently "taking my hand. Accepting my help" i said and like i reminded her she let go of my hand and stepped back only to be pulled in again by me she crushed in my chest and flinched at her wounds i stared at her eyes not noticing that my hand was squeezing her waist she flinched and put her hand on mine like reminding me of my hand.

I quickly pulled away noticing her hand on her waist what the have I done? Did i just hurt her!? Even if i did so what! I'm the Italian mafia boss after all this girl will not make me a soft person.

"we are going to your room" i said turning my back to her "my room?" she asked "yeah you are gonna stay her but not as a prisoner" i explained "now follow me" i said walking out of the cell

Loria pov

I was walking behind him out of the cell and into his house his house is massive i didn't see all of it. i just saw what we passed through the first floor and the second floor. the first because i went through it when i was out of the dungeon. It has his office in it and the second because it has* my room* in it.

I was feeling dizzy and tired i wanted to sleep for like 6 days straight my stomach hurts , my head, my rips. There were bruises in every inch of my body thanks to Daniel.

"this is your room" kai said opening a room has black walls, balck dressing room, a bathroom and a creamy bed "and what is the price?" i asked sitting on the bed "what do you mean?" he said leaning on the door "i mean what is the price? you can't just allow me to stay here after you beated me and got me full of bruises"i said. "if you are referring that I'm keeping you here so i can fuck you the answer is no I'm not interested in whores" kai said and i felt my cheeks burn. He turned his back to me and went out of the room.

I went to the bathroom took a very long shower and went to the dressing room i found some sweat pants and hoodies i took a black hoodie and wore it it was a very big one it reached to my knees is this a fucking joke? But i really don't give a shit about the size of it i went to the bed and once i laid my head on the pillow i went to sleep

I woke up on someone moving beside me i turned around to find some man in my bed he was taking off his pants what the hell is he gonna do?? I jumped from the bed and immediately regret it because the pain that i felt from my rips.

"what the fuck? What are you doing?" i asked the man my hand on my Ripa after i turned on the lights "come here you little whore and do your job" he said WHY DOES EVERYONE THINKS THAT I'M A WHORE??

Chapter 10

Loria pov

Why does everyone calling me a whore "I'm not a fucking whore" i yelled he got out of the bed and walked toward me "then what are you? An angel?" he asked sarcastically "stay were you are and don't you dare come close to me" i said stepping back "or what?" he said taking a step closer to me earning a bunch from me to his face.

"you little whore" he yelled at me taking my hair in his hands and slapping me i went straight to the floor and my nose started bleeding.

He was about to kick me in my stomach i looked him in the eyes and before he could deliver the kick to my rips i found someone stepping in front of me

"Cosa pensi di fare nik? " kai said looking at the man (What do you think you are doing nik?) "what? Is this little whore is a special whore to you?" the man said looking at me

I wasn't able to move my rips were on fire "out now" kai yelled at him. The man looked at the floor and then got out but before he could i heard his thoughts [Che diavolo era quello? Questa è la prima volta che mio fratello si preoccupa di una puttana] what?? HIS BROTHER? (What the hell was that? This is the first time my brother cares about any whore)

Kai pov

I looked at her she was on the floor her nose bleeding i think she has a broken rip or two because her hands were on her rips

"let me help you" i said leaning to her and giving her my hand she took it she looked like she was thinking of something she suddenly took a few steps away from me looking into my eyes with her gorgeous brown eyes.

"what the fuck? This man is your brother?" she asked how the hell did she know that i didn't think about it and even if i did i was covering my mind with that memory "how did you know that?" i asked taking a step towards her she took a step back well that's new "i heared him" she explained "why are you and your people doing this to me? Don't you see that Daniel already beated the hell out of me? Isn't that enough?" she yelled

Well she is breaking down "i didn't tell him to do that to you he must have thinks that you are.." "a whore" she said " I'm 17 idiots " she continued "so what? There is a lot of whores that are even younger" i yelled back at her i have had enough she can't just yell at me and disrespect me I'm kai lionail the Italian mafia boss

"fuck you and your mafia i don't give a shit about that" she said "don't you dare disrespect me you little whore" i said grabbing her neck "I'm not a whore I'm a virgin dumbass" she said trying to take her breath i released her from my grip and looked at her she was breathing hard she put her hands on her heart and looked at me and then she passed out

Loria pov

I opened my eyes to see that I'm in a different room I'm in a bed there is someone on the sofa infront of me but i can't see him my vision is blurred i closed my eyes and went to sleep

A few hours laterI opened my eyes to find that there is no one in the room now i tried to go out from the bed but my rips didn't help me

"don't move or you will pass out again" i heared someone saying i turned my head to see the blonde guy that was with Kai i think his name is arma "what happened?" i asked "well i Don't actually know" he frowned "why are you keeping me her?" i asked "I'm not" he said "i think kai forgot to introduce me. I'm arma" he said offering his hands for me to shake "I'm loria" i shaked his hands "now why does kai keeping me her? And why did kai's brother tried to rape me?" i asked

He looked at me without saying anything "Βασικά δεν ξέρω γιατί ο Κάι σε κρατάει εδώ" wait a minute his lips didn't move that means that this is what he thinks (I actually don't know why kai is keeping you here) but wait a minute how did i understand what he said he is talking greek "can you take me to him!" i asked "yeah i can but i don't think that it's a good idea" he said looking at the window to avoid eye contact with me "where is him?" i asked "i don't know" he said he is surely lying i can try to focus on his mind to know where he is

I looked at his eyes making eye contact he tries to avoid it many times "are you trying to read my mind?" he asked oh shit i can't let him know that "no i already tried in the cell and that didn't work did it?" i said looking him in the eyes he looked at me like he is trying to find out if I'm telling the truth or not and then i heared it [Δεν μπορώ να σου πω ότι είναι στο γραφείο του είπε ότι δεν σε ήθελε στα μάτια του για 24 ώρες.] well here it is (I can't let you know that he is in his office he said that he didn't want you in his eye sight for 24 hours)

"i need to go to my room can you help me?" i asked him "yeah sure" he said offering me his hand

He helped me to go to me room and to my surprise there wasn't any guards on the door i thought that he will put guards on my door to Stop me from runing away

"stay in your room. Your lunch and medicine are going to be delivered to you in their time" arma said and left i think it's the time i waited for 5 minutes and then opened the door and went straight to the office i know where the office is i have a good memory i knocked on the door and waited

"Entra" he said i opened the door to reveal a very angry kai "why are you here? Who told you that I'm in here?" he asked standing up from his chair and coming towards me "no one i don't need anyone to tell me i think you forgot about the mind reading thing" i said looking at his eyes [Non guardarmi così o non sarò in grado di trattenermi] (Don't look at me like that or i will not be able to hold myself)

"hold yourself to do what?" i asked "to do this" he said and then his lips met mine

DID I JUST HAD MY FIRST KISS WITH A MAFIA BOSS?

DID I JUST HAD MY FIRST KISS WITH A MAFIA BOSS?

Chapter 11

Loria pov

His lips were soft on mine and the kiss was a very good kiss or not i don't think that i will know if it is not its my first kiss after all

I broke the kiss and took a step back from him he looked me in the eyes "what the hell?" i asked he was looking at me i tried to read his mind but i couldn't he was blocking his fucking mind "what?" he asked "you just kissed me?" i said "and?.. What? You didn't like it!" he said sarcastically "no i didn't and don't you dare do it again" i said and went straight to the door

"Non osare fare un altro passo" he said calmly (Don't you dare take another step) "why? I don't understand why I'm here in the first place and I'm sure as hell don't know why you just kissed me" i said turning to him "I'm kai lonail I'm..." "yeah yeah the fucking mafia boss i know and i said i didn't give a shit didn't i?" i interrupted him

He gave me a death glare and came towards me slowly taking step by step without breaking eye contact i stood still where i was standing not looking anywhere but his eyes

" Perché pensi di essere speciale? "he asked (Why do you think that you are special?)" Non lo sono, ma non ti la farò umiliare "i said back in his own mother language (I'm not but I'm not going to let you humiliate me)" why do you keep making a big deal out of the kiss? " he said standing in front of me he was so close to me i swear if I moved an ench we will be kissing again" maybe because i didn't want you to kiss me" i said "and why is that? every girl would die to a kiss from me" he said " i wonder why" i said

He took a step back from me "well it won't happen again" he said "thank you" i said and left his office

Kai pov

I don't know what is this girl doing to me no other girl ever dared to say something to me. She wasn't even supposed to be in here. I was dealing with vulian's problem and sending him to other warehouse so they won't meet before she came in.

"kai are you available?" arma asked while entering the office "Sì arma entrare" i said (yes arma come in) he sat down infront of me he was thinking of something like he didn't know how to tell me "what arma? Say it" i said while looking in the papers infront of me "well i was going to say that.." he was interrupted by nik entering the office without even knocking "Cos'è successo ieri fratello? Mi hai appena urlato davanti a qualche puttana." he yelled standing infront of me (What happened yesterday brother? You just yelled at me infront of some whore) "control yourself nik and she is not a whore" i said not looking from the paper i was dealing with "then what is she? A special whore" he said sarcastically "i said control yourself I'm not going to say it again don't forget who you are talking to" i said calmly

"calm down nik" arma tried to calm him but nik just kept yelling "stay out from it arma I'm talking to my brother" "enough" i yelled looking at nik "what do you want nik?" i asked Leaning back to my chair "i want to know why you yelled at me infront of your whore yesterday" he said "she is not a whore" i yelled "and don't you dare say another word" i continued "she is the girl from abria nik" arma explained "what girl?" he asked

How could he know that? he knew nothing about abria in the first place how could he knew about loria!"you wouldn't know because you were never here in the first place so keep doing whatever you are doing and stay away from her" i said standing up and out from the office

I went to the gym i found her there what the fuck is this girl doing she is sick she has a broken rips who even allowed her in here

"who told you that you can enter this gym! " i said looking at her she was wearing my T-shirt it was reaching up her knees and leggings she was bunching the bunch bag she turned to me once she listened to what i said

"i didn't know That you need a permission" she said "well now you know" i said leaning to the wall "i already finished" she said taking the water bottle and the towel and was passing by me i held her arm "you are injured you shouldn't train" i said avoiding eye contact with her "I'm. But I like training" she said taking a sip from the water bottle "where did you learn that? Abria doesn't have a gym" i asked her now looking at her eyes "i always worked out without a gym and i have always wanted to learn boxing and fighting" she said looking at the bunch bag behind her

I can teach her "why would you do that?" she asked "do what?" i said she rolled her eyes shit mind reading "yeah shit" she said smiling she has an amazing smile i think i like seeing her smile she smiled even wider control your mind kai "i didn't say that i will i just said that i can" i said trying to change the subject and blocking her from my mind and i think it worked "well you are good" she said "of course I'm" i said she rolled her eyes again and was leaving but i held her arm tighter she looked at my hand that was holding her arm and then looked at my eyes her brown eyes were so fucking beautiful i wanted to kiss her again so bad

"don't even think about it" she said how? I'm blocking her from my mind with that memory "I'm not going to" i said taking a step back from her and leaving her arm she was about to leave the gym "why? " i asked her "because you already took my first kiss and i have had enough from you i have enough broken rips and bruises i don't want anymore" she said "your first kiss?" i asked but she was already gone.

Chapter 12

K ai pov

"boss your father wanted to talk to you" loca said

I was in my office working on some papers i didn't finish yet about the project "you can go loca" i said dismissing him he went out of the office

What does my father want now? Isn't it enough that he already wanted to kill loria I'm still not over it. after i took Daniel to my office he already told me everything but of course not without some extra details and he was taken care of i was really mad. He was my right hand for 2 years i trusted him. but i didn't tell my father that i knew anything

I went to my father's office "Hai chiesto di me.!" i. Said (you asked for me) "yes, sit down kai" i sat down infront of him "can you tell me why this girl is here for?" he asked "she can be useful" i said i want this conversation to end as soon as possible I'm already angry with him "how?" he asked taking a sip from his coffee "this is for me to know father" i said i can't tell him about the things that she can do certainly not until i know why he ordered to kill her "don't forget who you are talking to son" he said "with all my respect father you are the one that don't know who you are talking to" i said calmly looking him in the eyes "Cos'hai appena detto?" he said (what did you just say?) i looked at his face he was angry but i don't give a shit "i said that you don't know who you are talking to. Don't forget that I'm the mafia boss you are the one that gave me this title and i didn't forget what you did to me and my siblings when we were younger." i said and stood up ready to leave his office

My father was always mad at us with no reason he is the one that made me this cruel he was also a cheater he cheated on my mother so many times and my mother never asked for a divorce she knew that he won't allow it he was the Italian mafia boss he is the reason why i didn't chose a lover or a girlfriend since i was a teen. i was scared that i sill cheat on her or beat her or do anything that will harm her like him.

"kai we need you now" Arma said entering my office quickly i went after him to the meeting room "what is the issue?" i asked my men after i walked in "the Russians" loca said yeah it is a problem. a big one "what about them!" i asked looking at Arma "they somehow knew about the project and the girl" arma explained "how??" i asked angirly "we don't know yet" nik said entering the meeting room i looked at him my little brother just joined the meeting that's news. "get max out of the project and call all the men to the weapon's room" i said walking away from them and out from the meeting room I need loria now

Loria pov

I was in my room laying in bed thinking of the meeting between kai and his father yes i was there by his eyes like i did with Daniel the problem is i don't know how i suddenly find myself seeing with someone's eyes without even trying to the mind reading I'm trying to control it now i practice alot but still there is some people i can't read their mind i don't know why but the question i was thinking of now what have kai's father done to him and his brothers.

"loria i want you now" kai said while entering my bedroom i straightened suddenly earning an ow from my rips to the sudden move "there is something called knocking" i said my hands on my rips i was wearing only his T-shirt now he was looking at me i tried to read his mind but couldn't "let me tell you what's on my mind and saving this part i was thinking of your fabulous body in my T-shirt" he said

Wow this guy have balls "but it's not it's time now i want you in the weapon's room now" he said "okay let's go" i said standing from the bed walking towards the door he blocked me "what?" i asked "you are going to the weapon's room with all my men inside only with my T-shirt?" he said looking at my legs shit i forgot i took a step back from him "of course not" i said walking to the dressing room i grabbed a white hooded sweatshirt and a leggings and went out to find him still in my room

"i could have find the weapon's room alone" i said "yeah yeah i know now let's go" he said holding the door to me

We were in the weapon's room all his men were here i only recognized arma, Loca and his dumbass brother nik "i want you to read their mind and tell me who may have snitched something to the Russians" kai said "with all my respect. my mind reading thing is not working on all the people for god know why" i said sarcastically " try" kai said i looked at the first one infront of me he was loca his mind was full of wondering how can i do that and a movie scenes, second one was nik he was thinking of my fucking body and why his brother have interest in me i knew that kai never date anyone he would only choose some whores to fuck, third one was Arma he was thinking of food i think we are gonna be a very good friends he also thinks that i can't read his mind so he was thinking of kai and why he care for me he shipped us in his mind and list goes on and on. There are people i couldn't read their mind for god knows why and after alot of time i was finished and tired.

"so you tell me that there is alot of people that you can't read their mind" kai said confused "yes" i answered "and all you can't read their mind are ones that you didn't deal with" he said again "yes" i said looking into his eyes he looked at me and to some other man "come with me" he said "I'm really tired kai and.." "come with me" he interrupted me and held his hand to me i took it and he led me to some guy that i already tried to read his mind "touch him" he said "what?" i looked at him confused "just do it" he said taking my hand and put it on him and i could read his mind.

I looked at kai "what? Did it work?" he asked i was focused on the man that i was reading his mind he was thinking of how i angry him and how he want me gone and something else he was looking at the clock behind me "when those fucking Russians are gonna come this stupid whore can read my mind anytime soon" i pulled away from him "kai the Russians are gonna come here" i said looking to him and then there were bullets everywhere.

Chapter 13

K ai pov

There were bullets outside loria was standing beside me looking at the men that was taking weapons and guns from the weapon's room and going outside she didn't flinch at the bullets sound gared was trying to run but nik was after him i didn't think for a second that gared would be a traitor or that he can sell us to the Russians but he did

"come with me" i said holding her hand "where are we going? " she said i took her out from the weapon's room while she was behind me i shot some people that were in the house already not leaving her hand "kai we can't go back to your room" she said she knew the road to my room. "why?" i asked while taking cover "there is alot of men there" what? How did she know that i looked into her eyes " don't you dare think that I'm with gared" she said "there is alot of bullets voices coming from your room" she said i was amazed how is this woman keep amazing me like this! "we don't have a time for you to fantasy me use your fucking brain what are we gonna do? " she said "to my office" i said standing up and started shooting at some men that were in the way.

I opened my office's door to find Arma in there he was trying to get max out from the project max can help us in this situation he is good at creating bombs that can buy us some time to go to the dungeon i was still holding loria's hand and to my surprise she was holding my hand back she didn't pull away from me but she suddenly pulled her hand away from me and held her head.

"are you okay?" i asked she wasn't responding she wasn't even looking at us "she is seeing with someone's eyes kai" Arma explained "how did you know?" i asked "i was with her once" he said and continued what he was doing. I looked at her now her eyes were closed she was squeezing her eyes.

" hey hey you are gonna be okay "i said putting my hand on her face pulling her to my chest she opened her eyes and there was confusion in her eyes.

"what? What did you see loria?" i asked"your father" she said and then passed out

Loria pov

"you can't just leave me here you have to take me with you so they think that i died. If they didn't i will be dead" jurai lionail said "i will. but not now. Right now we will have to just put a bullet in your arm and go" some man said to him holding his gun to jurai's shoulder and he pulled the trigger.

I opened my eyes breathing heavily and coughing i found myself at kai's office. Kai looking at me his hand on my back and instead of arma i found max he was doing something with chemicals.

"are U okay! What happened? You were talking about my father what happened to him ?" kai said talking fastly and looking to me "your father is with the Russians" i said. max looked at me confused. of course he is. he don't know any thing of those new powers. "what do you mean? How did you find out?" max asked "it's a long story max just focus on what you are doing" kai said standing.

I stood up only to fall again but before i could hit the ground kai hold me.

"look where are you going I'm not going to be here all the time to catch your ass from falling" kai said tightening his grip on my rips i flinch. my rips are still aching and now my head too i think it's from using too much power i don't have any left. I looked into his eyes and said "can you take your hand away from my fucking rips i didn't ask you to catch me you could have left me to fall" i said.

His hands left my waist and i collapsed into the ground " you deserved it" max said chuckling "it's not funny" i said angrily "enough you two max can you focus on the grenade in your hands?" kai said firmly giving me his hand to take. I refused and was still siting on the floor "you won't need it" i said they looked at me confused "the Russians are not going to come in here they are just playing with you, with the help of your father of course" i said kai looked at me with cold emotionless face.

" i still don't know how you know that" max said "long story short i have super powers and i don't know how" i said standing up "could it be from the door she broke when she left!" max said looking at kai "what do you mean?" kai said turning his full attention to him.

"i mean that when she left abria she broke the door to this world and that's why i couldn't leave because the power that we put in the door wasn't there and the door was broken. when Arma found out he got another source of power to provide the door's city with it and that's how i came out" max explained i didn't understand a word."does that mean that you have superpowers too?" i asked "no loria because i didn't break the door i only went through it" he said

Kai was looking at the small forest that contains some houses and markets in it that i think is abria i felt a strong ache in my head and rips i felt like my whole body was on fire

" this is too much " i said siting on the chair with my head in my hands " are you okay?" kai said "i..." i was interrupted by Arma opening the office's door and coming in "the Russians have left but your father is wounded" arma said

Kai looked at me [how? Didn't you say that he was with them?] i heared kai's mind i think he wants me to hear this

"yes kai and he even asked to go with them but the man didn't accept" i explained

Why am i feeling like he don't trust me "i don't trust you" he said. Well i guess that i was right "if you don't want to then don't I'm not telling you to trust me I just told you what I saw" i said coldly if he don't trust me then fuck him i don't care it's not my mafia or anything

I stood up and left the office only to be grapped by some man "Тишина" (silence) i didn't listen i screamed i found kai, Arma and max out from the office and in front of me

"i don't think that you want to do this you won't go out in one piece if anything happened to her" kai threatened going to his gun "hey hey put your hands where i can see it or she will pay" the Russian man said aiming his gun to my waist why does anyone just keep squeezing on my rips I flinched "oh she is already hurt. How about we just play with her for a bit!" he said grapping my waist and squeezing on my rips "Ah. Stop" i said but of course he choose to ignore it squeezing even harder "Ahh. I said stop you are hurting me" i said squeezing my eyes shut from the pain

"oh! Am i?" he said grinning "if you just squeezed her one more time i will cut your hand and shove it up to your ass" kai threatened "oh! And How about this" he punched me in the rips and i fell into the floor.

Chapter 14

K ai pov

Loria was on the floor holding her rips there is blood i don't know from where but she is bleeding she didn't look at me she was squeezing her eyes shut i think it's from the pain the Russian man was holding a gun to her threatening arma to put the gun he was holding to his head down or he will shoot her max was standing next to me his eyes are full of anger he was looking at her.

"enough" i said "what are you here for?" i asked him "for her" he said "that's impossible" i said. He kicked her and yelled a 'put the gun down' sentence "arma put the gun down" i told him "what? What do you mean? He is holding his gun to her head she is under our protection and you are telling me to put the gun down!" arma yelled

Uhh i hate when people yell at me "PUT THE FUCKING GUN DOWN" i yelled not breaking eye contact with the russian man i saw that he got frightened from my voice GOOD "don't put it down arma" max said taking a step forward earning the russian man to undo the saftey of the gun and ready to pull the trigger "what the fuck are you doing? Get back to where you were standing" i told max"no, I'm not gonna stand her watching her dying" max said

"enough! just pull the god damn trigger man and end this shit" she screamed opening her eyes looking at the man

"don't test me Красивый and don't you dare raise your voice at me or i won't hesitate i will kill you right now with cold blood" the man said Turning his full attention to her "you are bluffing." she said "i know That you are afraid and you don't have the balls to pull this trigger, or even if you have them why do you think that you are scaring me? i have nothing to lose I'm already a prisoner here atlest if you killed me i will be set free" she continued (beautiful)

What is she doing! I don't think that she know that this man is a fucking mafia and he could end her life right away

"man what is she doing!" arma whispered to me "i don't fucking know" i said "she is detracting him" max explained "Tι! She is insane if she thinks that she can fool him" arma said "i don't think so" max said (What!)

I took the chance to take a few steps closer to them because his attention was all to her well that's a mistake. i grapped his hand pulling it behind his back he pulled the trigger it didn't hit me i took the gun from his hand and threw it away he was under my mercy now i can easily kill him in this position his hands behind his back his head leaning down submitting to me

"you know that i can kill right now don't you? " I asked "Да, but you won't" he said shaking underneath me "you are right i won't" i said he released a heavy breath i don't think he knows what i will do "but i will do what i promised" i continued "what do you mean?" he asked his voice is not as powerful as before he has a shaky voice now "didn't i say that if you touched her one more time i will cut those hands of yours and shove them up to your ass?" i said smiling a devilish smile he was still as a dead body not even breathing "well what man would i be if i broke my promise!" i said smirking

Loria pov

I was laying on the floor holding my rips max beside me looking to kai arma was standing right next to him waiting for him to say the word to take the man's life but instead the word was "give me your knife arma" he was waiting for the knife to cut the man's hands i now know that his name is micha

I think they know that he will do it because they weren't surprised they were looking at him waiting. well now i know that kai's promise never broke

I watched as he took the knife ready to cut his hands but i shut my eyes i don't want to see this but instead i heared it i heared the man screaming begging for mercy but kai never gave it to him

"take him and his hands to the dungeon we will get to the shove it up to your ass later" kai said

I opened my eyes to see micha now with no hands his hands are with arma and max was holding the man to take him to the dungeon

Kai came to me examining my rips without touching {how is she bleeding!} i heared his thoughts "well i don't know either so will you help me go to a doctor or will you leave me her to die bleeding?" i said looking at him he didn't say a word he grapped me gently trying not to touch my rips or hurt me Aww this version of kai is cute he is concerned about me

"why are you smiling?" he asked not looking at me in his arms "I'm not" i said straightening my face to show no emotion "you know that you are a terrible lier right?" he said "well i was thinking that it's a cute thing you worrying about me" i said smirking he stopped moving suddenly hitting my rips to his chest "Ahh, dude you can't just stop moving suddenly" i said my hands on my stomach "I'm not worried about you" he said "yeah yeah sure" i said he put me down harshlyThis man is going to kill me "well if you think that i am worried about you then that's my answer. you can go to your room alone i will go to my office and tell someone to tell the doctor" he said turning his back to me "i don't understand why you didn't leave the man to kill me and end this shit" i said trying to move slowly holding to the walls beside me

I was still walking slowly to my room my rips was on fire and i now know what is bleeding. when i fell on the floor when the man punched my rips there was a broken glass it sank to my right i didn't take it off because that will be stupid thing to do i will just bleed more

I found kai in front of me leaning towards the wall with his eyes closed "i thought that you might need my help with the stairs" he said "you thought wrong" i said trying to open my eyes i was sleepy but i know that it's from the blood loss he opened his eyes looking to me and i saw regret in it [shit i wasn't supposed to leave her. she looks like she will pass out] i heared his thoughts and i decided to ignore it i don't have enough power to talk he walked to me and left me off the floor he carried me bridal style my right was slammed to his chest"Amm.." i tried to not make a sound but it hurts the glass sanked deeply into my right

He looked at me searching for the reason to this sound "put me down i can make my way to my room alone you do nothing but damage" i said "what was that sound? i didn't touch your rips" he said confused

I didn't replay he walked to my room with me in his arms then put me on bed. he is supposed to leave now why is he standing right next to me?

"you know that you can leave now right?" i asked he didn't reply to me he was searching for the bleeding source "it's my right" i said. why did i say that? Why was i feeling guilty because i didn't tell him before! it's not like he cares. in a second he was crouching to my right side examining it "it's a broken glass" i continued why don't i shut the hell up!

"it sanks so deep" that was him "you will need to do a surgery" he said "I'm okay" i said. I'm not and he knows it so instead of talking to me he choosed to ignore it

My eyes was beginning to shut i have no power left "loria stay awake the doctor will finish my father and come to you as soon as possible just try to open your eyes and stay awake" he said

I'm not capable of opening my eyes I'm beginning to drift away and the last thing i saw before my eyes closes kai runing out of the room to call the doctor.

Chapter 15

K ai pov

She passed away afew hours ago i went straight to the doctor to tell him to stop what he is doing and come to her he was stitching my father so he left it to someone else to continue and came with me to her biru was the only doctor that i trusted he was with me years ago when my father was beating the hell out of me. He was beating us all but to me it was extra beating because i never shut my mouth i was cursing him even when he is beating me so he got even more angry and beat me more and harder if my mother was in state that she can't bear anymore beating i would do trouble so he would leave her and come to me so the only doctor i trusted was biru he was always fixing me after.

He told me that she is stable now her wounds will heal but it will leave a scar because it was so deep and about her rips she will be okay but she will take time and for now he just left her to rest

"I want all the camera videos in my father's office" i ordered nik when he came back after he dealed with the traitor i want to make sure is she saying the truth or not." Sì, Capo" he said and went out from the meeting room i gave the rest of my men the new instructions about the house's safety and dismisses them i have to go to arma to check on the project i haven't checked on it for a long time

"how is it going arma?" i asked him when i entered the office "it's good" he said but why does i feel that he is lying "but loria's mother is so sad and angry she didn't go to the farm since she left" he continued even when she is out she is a trouble "and what are we gonna do about this?" max asked entering the office "Δεν ξέρω" arma said (I don't know)

I think there is only one solution "we have to send her to her mother" i said i know that i need her by my side but it's for the best "what? And what if anything happened to her the people in abria never been exposed to this power twice" arma explained "he is right, she only exposed to the power once and she can read minds and those other things you told me about what will happen if she went through the door again and not once but twice" max continued "and who said that she will go through the door twice?" i said "what do you mean?" max asked "it means that she will go back to abria forever" i said

Loria pov

I opened my eyes coughing and breathing heavily what is he gonna do?? He can't send me away to abria again i finally came out of it i was there with them. i saw them taking about me returning to abria i don't approve they can't do that i have to talk to kai

I came out from the bed slowly careful not to hurt my rips i got a shirt from the dressing room it was a very big shirt i had to pull the sleeves up and wore nothing underneath it i went to the office where i saw them talking my feet are bare because i couldn't find my shoes or any other shoes that are my size i opened the office's door to find only arma inside he looked at me with wide eyes

"what are you doing here? And why you don't wear any pants?" he asked "it's not like i found any. Where is kai?" i asked "he is at the gym" he said i closed the door behind me and went to the gym i could hear arma yelling at me from behind but i ignored him

I was at the gym i looked at him he wasn't wearing any shirt only a black sweat pants he didn't see me her i think he is thinking of something i can try to focus on his mind especially now that he don't know I'm here to read his mind [i don't know what I'm going to do with her. I can't send her away, i can't live without her i don't know why. I was never like that with any other woman]

i was interrupted by coughing i think i don't have enough power i was holding my rips because of the hard coughing was aching my rips

he turned to me looking surprised i would die to know what is he thinking now but i don't have the power

"what are you doing here?" he asked moving closer to me he was boxing without gloves his hands were so red and bruised "i was searching for you" i said he came to me and lift his hand to my nose there was blood on his hand am i bleeding!! "why are you not in your bed?" he asked "I'm searching for you" i said he was looking at my body "why are you wearing my shirt?" he asked while trying to remove his eyes from my body "oh is that yours?" i asked now blushing i bite my bottom lip he looked at my lips and moved away from me

"why were you searching for me?" he asked "i want to talk to you" i said "about?" he asked still looking at the floor "why are you walking with bare feet?" he interrupted when i was about to talk " i couldn't find my shoes" i said he lift me to his chest and carried me bridal style

"put me down please" i said "i will not put you down so stop struggling or you will hurt yourself" he said

He took me to my room and gently laid me on my bed "don't leave your bed or you will hurt yourself" he ordered and turned to leave

"kai i want to talk to you" i said straightening on the bed "about what?" he asked turning to me "about you sending me back to abria" i said looking at his eyes i saw shook "how?" he asked "i was there" i said "yeah sure it's a really stupid question from me to ask" he said

It is actually he already know that i can see with someone's eyes he saw me doing it once and blah.. Blah.. Blah

He was staring at me because i was still in his shirt i could feel his breath on my face he was so close his breath was so hot his hand traveled to my waist i looked at his hands moving from my waist to my ass my heart was beating so fast i could hear it loud and clear and I'm sure he hears it too "stop" i said he looked at my eyes i was trying so hard not to kiss him right now he licked his lips starring at my lips [stop kai control yourself you can't do that she don't want to. But it's so fucking hard with her in only my shirt her body was driving me crazy i can feel my dick hardening] "STOP" i yelled taking a step away from him and holding my head

He looked at me and i can see his dick hardening through his pants i blushed "STOP!" i yelled again this was for me and my mind to stop thinking about his fucking dick

"U okay?" he asked me i opened the door and got out from the room i have to stop he is not good to me and of course not those ideas

"hey watch where you going" a tall muscled man said to me i ignored him and was leaving when he grapped my arm squeezing it "i didn't hear your apology" he said looking at me he was really beautiful he has brown hair, brown eyes and a little brown beard that was looking recently cleaned there isn't any hair not in it's place " it's rude to stare" he said getting angry at me.

"take your hand away from me" i said "or what?" he asked i looked into his eyes [this bitch better apologize now or I'm killing her right now in this place] i heared his thoughts "you will wait for eternity" i said.

He looked at me "what?" he asked "i will not apologize because it's you who was on his phone and it's you who bumped into me so it's you who should be sorry" i said.

[i think this mouth of hers is gonna be so good around my..] "Stop" i said holding my head with my other hand "stop what!" he asked.

I have no power to talk or think or anything and my mind keep reading his fucking mind i just want it to stop "Ahh" i felt my head aching and my eyes was starting to drift this is not happening again.

And then i passed away.

Chapter 16

K ai pov

Why did she went out like that what happened? I didn't follow her to give her space but I'm seriously worried so i sent max he is her friend after all she knows him for some time before us and most importantly she trust him

"dude we can't send her to abria" max said entering the office "and why is that?" i asked closing my laptop and looking at him "she is sick. Her power is overwhelming her and we can't expose her to the x rays again"He said angrily

I know that she is sick but if she didn't get back to abria she will be in more danger and so is the project i will not accept that my project will just fall apart i spent a lot of time and a lot of money on it.

"loria will go to abria and that's it we are not going to talk about it one more time" i said firmly "Έχει δίκιο, η Κάι Λόρια μόλις πέθανε στην αγκαλιά του Κουρ" arma said entering the office (he ia right kai. Loria just passed out in kur's arms) "what?? Where is she?" i asked standing from my chair "she is in her room max took her to it and called the doctor he said that she must rest" arma explained.

I was about to get out from the office but arma holded my hand "Πρέπει να ξεκουραστεί" arma told me (She must have some rest). I shoved his hands away and got out from the office i went straight to her room but i didn't get in i just waited outside i wanted to see her so bad but this is not right. She is making me weak and i can't be weak and I'm a small version of my father I'm hurting her. I used to hate my father for doing that to my mother and i promised myself that i will never be like him and that's what I'm doing now. I'm hurting her even if it's not on purpose

"i can hear your thought kai don't think That if you are outside my room that i won't be able to hear you" loria yelled from inside the room

I opened the door and went inside blocking my mind this time with a song that i like i can't pretend that i wasn't out she caught me. She smiled when she saw me

"look me in my eyes tell me every thing is not fine and the people ain't happy or the river has run dry" she sang "you know it" i said setting beside her on the bed "yeah it's one of my favorites actually" she said "look since you already heared what i thought then you know that you must go to abria and it's not something to discuss about" "you are not like your father" she interrupted me "funny. You don't know anything about me and I'm not willing to tell you anything about me neither so just keep the space." I said firmly

She looked at the walls behind me i know that she is thinking about what is she gonna tell me to convice me to let her be here." I'm going to leave " she said

What? She is not going to convice me! She is not going to do anything? She just accepted it like that! "good i will tell arma to prepare the door for you" i told her and went to the door "but I'm not going back to abria" she said making me stop walking and turning back to her "What?" i asked " you heared me" she said.

Loria pov

Why do i feel that i don't want to go! it's not an option i will go no matter what happens he don't want me here and i didn't get out from abria just to get hurt and go back to it. i haven't done anything yet and if i got back to abria there is no way that i will be able to get back here they will make sure of that.

"what do you mean?" he asked looking angry " i mean That i will go. You don't want me here but i will not go back to abria i just came out of it" i said "i didn't ask for your opinion" he said and turned to leave " and I'm telling you that i will not go back to it whether you like it or not" i said firmly.

He went out from the room and closed the door behind him. And i felt pain in all my bruises and broken rips without knowing what is the pain's source.

"Hey" arma said opening the door and entering "Hi" i said smiling to him. Arma is a really good person i really started to like him. " how are you doing?" he asked me "good" i said "kai told you?" he asked again looking at the floor "actually i told him" i said "you told him? Told him what?" he asked now looking confused "that i will go" i said "loria you can't go back the power will make you damaged you won't be able to Differentiate between consciousness and subconscious" " I'm not going to abria" i interrupted him " what? Then where?" he asked "i don't know yet but i will go anywhere. I will start searching for my father." i said he looked at me Surprised.

"why do you want to search for him! . He left you" he said "i want to know why" i said looking at my fingers remembering all my mother's talk about him " you don't know anything about the world out there loria" he said putting his hand on my knees "yes, but i will" i said

Kai pov

"max put some guards on her room she won't be able to come out of her room if i didn't tell her to. Kur tell your boss that she is not for sale and don't ever talk about her again. Nik bring me arma Now" i gave instructions to all the men so that she will not be able to get out from the house

"I'm not your stupid hoe so you give me instructions between your men and i didn't want to tell you that in front of them. So take care of your fucking tone when you are talking to me" kur said angrily

Kur is my cousin but his loyalty is to the Americans when my mother married my father they made an alliance my mom was the daughter of the Americans and they just sold her to my father so they can get money and alliance in their war with the Russians but instead the Russians turned to be our enemy and left the Americans so it became a problem to my father's head that's why he kept hurting my mom because he thought that she is the one that made this problem.

"kur. If i was you I would have took a very good care of every word that's coming out of my mouth or i will take your tongue out" i told him "you are threatening me for the second time kai. The first was because of your stupid whore and that's the second. So Be careful" he said. It's the last thing that i will ever care about. The Americans are so weak they even don't have weapons they are taking it from us "you know that i never threat" i said " you are always threatening" kur said "so how about i show you!" i told him getting up from my chair "Stai bluffando " kur said (You are bluffing)

"Vi prometto che non lo è. Ti dico se esperienza l'ho anche visto tagliare le mani di qualcuno, e senza esitazione" loria said entering my office (I promise you that he is not. I tell you of experience i even saw him cutting someone's hands, And without hesitation)

"wow you are so sexy when you are talking Italian" kur told her. She looked at him while takinga few steps towards max who was setting on the sofa "you know That i can read your mind right?" she asked him. He nodded his head "and still you are imagining all those fucking pictures" she said and looked at him with disgust. I looked at him with anger in my eyes. He took a step towards her. She didn't move as usual. "what can i do! you are so beautiful" he said while still getting closer to her "beauty is dangerous maybe i use it to get you close to me and kill you" she said taking a step towards him until they became so close to each other. Arma looked at me whispering to me about calming down "you are full of shit just like your maker" kur told loria and put his hand on her waist just where the wound from the glass is. She flinched when he tightened his grip on her i was about to step between them when she started talking "you are right. I'm a lot like him. in fact I'm a women version of him". And then she took his gun from his waist band and pulled the trigger.

I looked at her. She has the gun in her hand looking at kur with an emotionless face. Kur was right she is just like me but not that bluffing part the cold one

I went to her and took the gun from her hand

"what have you done!" i said trying to make her feel guilty but i was proud. i know i shouldn't but i was "killed him" she said smoothly. "what the hell loria! You don't know what you have done." max said "what? Killing him!" she said turning her eyes from kur's body to max. Max looked at her then at me and Arma "what are we gonna do now?" he askedI looked at loria her hands were on her wound "take her to the doctor" i told max and turned to leave but she took a step in front of me blocking me from the door "NO" she yelled "be careful I'm not kur" i said moving her to the side but she grapped my arm "you will listen to what i have to say" she told me. I looked at her eyes "MOVE" i told her "NO" she said still not breaking eye contact. I shoved her away but instead of moving her to max's side i shoved her to the floor. She fell down on her right and whimpered arma went straight to her

"you okay?" he asked her. She didn't answer him i was standing still. She wasn't supposed to fall. I was supposed to move her to max's side and i just harmed her again. "you didn't harm me" she said trying to get up by using arma's hand. I looked at her and saw her struggling so i went to her. Carried her to the sofa and went to my chair.

"what do you want to talk about?" i asked. She looked at kur's body. His body was still on my office's floor "I'm not going to abria so you have two options the first is letting me go so i can find my father myself..." wait what? She is searching for vulian? Why she didn't tell me? But why would she? And why is she searching for him! he is supposed to be dead in abria. why is she still searching what have she found so that she start searching for him?

" so?" she interrupted my thinking "what?" i asked " you wasn't paying attention right?" she asked " no" i told her she looked at me with sadness in her eyes that i wasn't giving her attention or even listening to her.

"i was telling you that you have two options: the first is to let me go so i can search for my father alone. The second is you are letting me live her with you and helping me to find him" she said her hands are still on her wound

"the second" i told her without thinking. Shit i was suppose to think for even a five minute for God sake.

"but there is a condition" she said looking at my eyes "what?" i asked "you are going to teach me boxing, fighting and using guns" she said "clearly you don't need a lesson at using guns" i said pointing at kur's body "I'm not kidding" she said i looked at her. "okay" i said. "and what is it for me?" i continued "i will work with you" she said.

Chapter 17

L oria's pov

He was still like a statue looking at me nothing on his mind i couldn't hear anything from it. Arma and max standing with their body leaning on the wall thinking of kai's respond max was afraid that kai will have a respond that will make me go he wants me here. And arma was thinking about what if he let me work with them! It will make their mafia even stronger with no spy in it because i will be reading their minds and even i will see things they don't know about and that he will search for any thing about my powers and try to make me control it

"so?" i asked losing patience he has been thinking for like ten minutes "i agree with a condition" he said okay now I'm afraid his condition will make this more difficult and it could be impossible

"what is it?" i asked looking at his eyes "I'm the one that will train you" he said "i appr..." "wait, don't be stupid and listen to all of it" he said "okay continue" i said getting up from the sofa to be in a setting position max helped me

"i will be the one to train you, you will not do anything without my knowing, you will be with me all the time" he said "you finished?" i asked "yeah" he said resting his head on his hand leaning on the chair "i don't think that it would be a problem" i said "excellent" he said getting up "don't be stupid and listen to all of it" i said looking into his eyes to see his expression using his own words against him "smart" max said smiling arma was behind him trying to control his laugh kai in front of me "Stai giocando a un gioco pericoloso" that was kai's mind (You are playing a dangerous game) "Sono io?" i said (Am i?)

He Crossed his arms looking at me leaning on the wall waiting for me to continue "i don't see a problem in you training me but the opposite i see that i will be trained by the best, second is approved too i don't think that it will be a problem you will know either way from your bodyguards or your camera's system. Lastly i don't understand your third condition. You mean as an assistant?" i asked he was looking at me with his mind blocked." U finished?" he asked."yeah" i said

He moved towards me leaning down to be at my level his face is not so far from mine he let me in his mind seeing him kissing me "i told you that U are playing a dangerous game" i heared his mind

I moved my head back he looked at my eyes smirking and came towards me again now his mouth is so close to my ears "like a bodyguard" he said his voice soft. I could smell his cologne it was so good. It smells just like chocolate he then moved fast and in a minute he was leaning on the wall again

"so?" he asked i was still at my place can't move "Τι της είπες ότι είναι παγωμένη;" Arma said to kai smirking a little (What did you say to her she is frozen)Fuck you kai "okay" i said he looked at me smirking again

"the training starts at 5" he said walking away "what 5?" i asked there is no way he means 5 Am who in hell wake's up at 5 to train! "Am" he said in a duh way. Fuck how am i supposed to wake up this early?

Kai's pov

It is 4Am i woke up to take a shower. I love cold showers at 4 am. I took a shower, got a black sweatpants and white T shirt and went straight to her room. I didn't approve of her condition i will just make her go to abria willingly. I know that she hates to wake up early that's why i made the training at 5 i usually start training at 7. I just like waking up at 4 to get a shower, prepare my day at work and start my office work looking at the papers and everything.

I opened her door she was sleeping peacefully the clock was reading 4:45 I woke her up by cold water "what the Fuck!" she said getting up to a setting position on the bed "every time i come here and see you are not awake i will wake you up like this" i said putting the glass on the table close to the door. "You have 30 minutes to take a shower, wear your clothes and be at my training room" i said opening the door "it's 4:47" she said "so?" i said closing the door behind me and went straight to my training room

I was doing some cardeo when she entered the training room i looked at my timer she used 34 minutes "you are 4 minutes late" i said "consider it from the 10 minutes that i was supposed to take sleeping" she said taking a bottle of water she was wearing black shorts with my black t shirt her hair in a high ponytail

"come here" i said. She came to me and played cardio with me for 20 minutes then the running and last thing it was time for the punching bag she was punching the bag furiously like she was punching someone

"that's enough" i said but she didn't stop "loria" i said she didn't respond "LORIA" i yelled at her she kicked the bag one last time and looked at me. She was sweating her right is bleeding again that's from the kick she wasn't supposed to kick now the kicks were supposed to be after she healed

She was looking at me her face is blank her right is bleeding she wasn't aware of it. She was just focused on something behind me i turned to see kar kur's twin she must have thought that it was him

"go to arma" i told her "how?" she asked "GO TO ARMA" i said louder this time gaining her attention. She went past me and was getting past kar when he holded her arm "you are her!" he said looking at her "Yes" she said surprising me i thought that she won't speak from the shock. "you know that you killed me brother! " he said tightening his grip on her arm "your brother?" she asked.

Loria's pov

I was at the training room with kur holding my hand i don't know how i killed him kai said that they buried him how is he now in front of me?

"you are her!" he asked i read his mind to know that he is asking about the supernatural girl "yes" i said looking at him trying to reach any memory of how he is alive "you know that you killed my brother!" he said. What? Brother? There is two kur? "your brother?" i asked.

i felt a hand grap me from behind and then a wall in front of me. It was kai he was in front of me now looking at kur's brother "what are you here for kar?" he asked. Kar! They are twins "I'm here with kir to see the bitch that killed our brother" he said looking at me kai's shirtless back is covering all of me "kir is here too?" kai asked "yeah" he said. Who is kir?

"loria go to arma to see your wound" he said "and tell him that kir is here" that was his mind . He looked at me to make sure that i read his mind and i nodded my head letting go of his hand and moving from behind him through the training door to go to arma's room. His gaze was with me kur's twin was looking at me like he was about to pull his gun and fire but he moved his head to kai agian when kai started speaking i didn't pay attention to what he was saying i just went to arma's room

"arma" i said entering his room. He was sleeping on the bed bare chest with just his pants on "sorry i should have knocked" i said giving him my back to give him a chance to get dressed "what happened? Why your right is bleeding?" he asked while getting dressed "just the train" i said "i have something to say to you" i continued "turn around I'm done" he said.

I turned around to see that he is dressed in a black shirt he was buttoning his last button "kir is here" i said "what??" he said I'm sure that he heared me he was just shocked "why all of you are afraid of him? . I don't understand anything. Even kai was scared of him" i said "kai is not scared of him he is scared of what he will do" he said getting his phone and texting max telling him about it.

In a minute we were in kai's office all of us. Me, max, arma, kai, his mom, nik, kar and another one looks exactly like kar

"i missed you so much" his mom said to kar but kar didn't give her any love he just looked at her and then looked to the floor

Kai was setting on his boss chair, me beside him, arma and max beside me, his mother on the sofa kar and his other look alike on the chairs in front of the table and nik beside his mother on the sofa. That was the first time seeing his mother she looks exactly like them but with a soft sad eyes

"so you are the one that killed my brother?" kar's look alike said "yes" i responded earning kai to look at me with disturbance in his eyes. "I'm kir" he said putting his hand for me to shake.

No one knows that i need to touch the person to read his mind. the only one that knew this was gared and he is dead. So i need to touch him to be able to read his mind.

I took his hand to shake and i heard kai's mind (what are you doing?) i looked at him reassuring him that it's fine. "loria" i told kir.

"i wanna know what you want kir?" kai asked kir runing out of patience. "easy my brother's revenge" he said looking at me "and how do you plan to get it?" kai asked now looking at me too i looked at him and he turned his head "i have lots of ideas" kir said i looked at him reading his mind

He wants to take me with them to the Americans to know how am i like that, to do experiments on me to make an army with supernatural powers not just my ability but another abilities i was back from his mind to arma's hands behind my back helping me to stay still

"i would like to know one of those ideas" kai told kir "by marriage" he said

What the hell! this man is lying. "okay" kai said. What the fuck is he doing is he going to sell me?

Chapter 18

Loria's pov

He is selling me! Seriously he is not bluffing i wasn't able to read his mind but his eyes said it all i looked at arma he was confused not understanding if kai is being serious or not i looked at max he was furious i think he is not a fan of the idea. Yeah me neither buddy.

"so when is the marriage? " kir asked kai "tomorrow" he said firmly "well i will be seeing you all tomorrow" kir said standing and walking out from the office

We were standing still like a statue all of us even kai himself. non of us moved not even an inch

"you have a plan right?" arma asked him hoping that he was pluffing "to what exactly?" kai said turning his chair to face us "to the wedding" i said looking at him "yeah we should call the lawyer to prepare the paper work" he said moving his arm to get his phone i was faster i snatched the phone before he can take it "you have no idea what he is planning to do" i said "i don't want to" he said trying to take the phone from my hand i moved it away "kai think about it agian" max told him finally out of his silence "i don't think about anything twice" he said opening his plam looking at me "Il telefono loria. ORA" i heared his mind (the phone loria NOW). I looked at his eyes "i think you should obey" he said. I gave him the phone going out of the office.

"Non è consentito seniorina" the bodyguard told me (It's not allowed ms) "Ho solo bisogno di qualche minuto puoi venire con me mi siederò in giardino" i told him trying to convince him but he still didn't allow it (I just need a few minutes you can come with me i will just sit in the garden). "Lascia che lei sarò con lei" i heard him from behind me (Let her i will be with her) "si capo" and just with that the guard let me out.

I went out taking in all the oxygen, taking in the sun, the sky. I always loved the sky even in abria kai sat on the chair looking at my back i could feel his gaze on me "you won't escape. Are you?" he asked me "to where?" I said turning to look at him "anywhere" he said.

I sat on the grass "i won't. First i don't know anything here I'm new to this world. Second this won't be very smart of me to run and make all the mafias in the world come after me" i said "you are smart" he said looking at me. I layed on the grass with my eyes closed oh i missed that

"you don't know what he will do" i said "who?" he asked "kir" i said not opening my eyes "I don't care" he said. That silenced me i continued laying there not speaking. Not doing anything but laying with my eyes closed and enjoying the sun while i can.

"that's enough we should go inside I have some things to arrange" he said breaking my peaceful silence i opened my eyes looking at him he was standing beside the door holding it so it won't close "come on hurry up loria i really have lots of things to do" he said. I stood up going to him

Once we are inside i walked to my room i don't wanna talk to him or to anyone. Why i gave in this easily? Because i have nothing to do. If i ran away all the mafias will be after me because all of them will know about me if it's not from the Italians it would be from the Russians or the Americans. And i know nothing about the real world i only read about it in books. And lastly i don't have any money to go anywhere. So let's just face the reality i don't have anything and I'm not in a position to make any choice also there isn't any.

Late at night

I woke up to see that the house is dark only kai's office's light was on that means that kai is in his office

I left him be and went to the kitchen to grap a glass of water and i was shocked to see kai in the kitchen preparing a snack shirtless he is supposed to he in his office "didn't they teach you to not stare" he said i looked at his face to see him smirking "no they didn't" i said that made his smirk go wider

I went inside the kitchen grapped a glass and filled it with water "want a snack?" he asked "no" i said coldly not looking at him i finished my water and poured myself another to put it beside me so whenever i needed it i won't have to go the kitchen i was on my way out when he blocked the door with his body "move" I said not looking at him "looks like you forgot who you are talking to" he said moving my head up with his fingers "no, i didn't i just don't care" i said he smirked "you like to use my words against me don't you!" he said moving towards me i took a step back "what can i say I'm a Harry Potter fan! " i said still taking steps back till my back hit the wall "well how are you gonna get out now? With the magic blanket!" he said "who told you that i care to get out?" i asked him looking at his eyes "so you are trapped here in my arms and you like it?" he said "no, i just don't care there is a big difference" i said with my cold face and not caring tone he moved to the side to make me go. I tried to but he held my arm "what happened to you! You now obey me. That must have been kir's effect on you. Yeah my cousin have that kind of effect" he said.

"you are joking? You are so stupid if you think that he wants to do anything good. You have no idea what is inside his mind. You have no idea how he treats his fuck toys. You have no idea what i saw in his mind" i said. I'm furious right now and i need to go to my room. I shoved his hand away using his own training tricks and went to my room. Best thing to do is sleeping

The next morning

I woke up at 5 went to the training room there was no one here. Did he finished already? No I'm not that late I'm just on time

"you shouldn't train" he said coming out from the changing room "i don't think that i asked" i said "you forget too much i should start considering make an appointment with the doctor for you" he said wearing his boxing gloves and giving me mine "well I'm not free today i have a wedding" i said punching the bag in front of me "you must start to punch the sides. You only punch the front" he told me. I did what he said I was punching the punch bag so fast and hard I was about to kick it when he held me leg "no" he told me. I lowered my leg following his instructions.

A few hours later

I was finished. I took a shower and changed my clothes to a sweatpants of his and a hoodie i still have no clothes and i won't need them since I won't see the sun again kir will be here in one hour so i have like 50 minutes to say goodbye but i hate goodbyes. i guess i will just spend time with them

I went to the kitchen to prepare something to eat i found lots of options but i chose the safest one pasta with red sauce and meatballs

I started by boiling the water and putting the pasta in it. Then i prepared the sauce using tomatoes, oninos, vinger, garlic and the spices and then i put the meat balls in it and left it be cooked.

"wow what is that smell! " Arma asked coming towards the kitchen "pasta with red sauce and meatballs" I said "dude i love pasta" he said "yeah me too" i told him continuing cooking. "the pasta is almost done go get max" i told arma he sprented to the office. I'm gonna miss him

In five minutes they were infront of me setting on the table in the kitchen with their plates filled with the pasta i sat next to them after i put myself a plate

"it's so good" arma said "how did you do it?" arma continued "i love cooking and my mom was the best cook in the
city" i told them remembering my mother and the fights that
always happened between us. I miss her and i miss grams

"what is that smell?" kai said entering the kitchen "loria
made an awesome pasta" arma told kai "get yourself a plate
before we eat it all" max said looking at arma "what do you
mean? You mean that i will eat it all?" arma said "i didn't
say anything" max said lifting his arms in surrender "but
you meant that" arma continued "dude he didn't mean that
just continue the pasta will get cold" i told arma trying to
shush him.Kai grapped a plate and sat beside me. He took
a fork and looked at me amazed "this is so good. arma was
right" kai said "I'm always right" arma said "oh shut up man"
Max said "you shut up" arma argued "i will miss you" I said
laughing but no one heared me luckily.

We were in kai's office kir is setting on a chair beside him
is Kar, kai and the lawyer

"so sign here mr kir" the lawyer told him. He signed "you
too mr kai" he told kai giving him the paper. Kai looked at me
standing behind him. I wanted to see anything in his eyes,
wanted him to let me see what's on his mind, wanted to
tell him about all the bad things that he will do to me. But
i couldn't. He signed "congrats" the lawer said handing the
paper to kai and out from the office

"congrats kur you deserve her" kai said shaking kir's hand.
So that's it. I moved from behind kai's back only to be pulled
agian by him. he held me by my waist.

"look kai i know that she is your project but i don't like my wife to be touched by another man" he said grapping my arm roughly "tsk tsk tsk. I advice you to remove your hand" kai threatened "from whom?" kir said "from my *project*" kai explained moving me behind him

The door knocked. And a pretty girl walked in looking so much like me "let me introduce you. Lora your wife" kai said smiling.

Chapter 19

oria pov

I was looking at the beautiful girl from over kai's shoulder that was standing right across from us she looks so much like me. She has a brown long hair, brown eyes but she is skinner than me.

"what is that supposed to mean?" kir asked kai not looking away from the girl "that means congrats on your bride" he said "i signed the contract to loria not lora" he said now turning to face us his voice was calm but his eyes, his eyes are way too far from calming "nah, you signed the contract to lora" kai said confidently"is that some king of a joke?" kar asked finally out of his silence "what joke?" kai asked pretending to not understanding "we wanted loria not this stupid girl" kar said raising his voice.

Even I'm behind him i can feel his jaw tenses "no, actually as my memory helps me you just asked marriage you didn't say anything about whom."kai said. Before anyone can replay he continues " And i advise you to lower your voice or you will meet your brother soon" he told kar "are you threatening us?" kir asked looking at kai with now furious eyes "how many times i will have to tell you that i don't threat?i just do" kai said taking step forward.

i looked at the beautiful girl that was standing right across from us her expressions doesn't have any fear in them i looked at Arma he was looking confused means that kai didn't share that lovely info with him. I looked at the girl agian focusing on her.

"dude just accept that you have no other choice and take me" i heared her mind. Why does she Want to go with him so much! How she is not even scared! And how can i read her mind. She must be someone that i dealed with. Who is she?

"don't look at me like girl I'm trying to help you i know that you can read my mind" i heared again. Okay so who is she? I don't even know how I'm going to ask her that without them knowing?

"so where that lead us?" kir asked still calm as before "leads to you taking your bride and going to your house" kai said. I looked at the girl again confused at how is she accepting that.

"I'm Kristina loria relax and don't think about it too much your nose is bleeding" i heared her thoughts then put my hands on my nose finding blood i removed the blood fast so that no one can see me. Kristina she is kai's right hand why is she doing that? Does she knows what he is about to do? And even worse because now he is angry too.

My head starts spinning as i saw her in his basement covered with bruises someone standing infront if her with a proud expression on his face like he is proud of what he has done to her. I put my hand on kai's back to help me standing straight because i feel like my knees starting to become weak. What was that? Am i seeing the future now? Or is it just because I'm scared of what he will do to her?

Arma sensed my weaknesses but didn't move. I sensed kai moving but my head was spinning i couldn't focus on why or where he is moving i closed my eyes for a while i can't let her do that she will get hurt. I have to do something but what should i do?

Kai pov

Of course I'm not giving them loria. But i can't refuse either because also the Americans are so weak kir isn't. Kir is not the American's boss but he is so dangerous. He loved making people's life hell he just enjoys it so i had to think.

*Flashback*I was at my office with max and Kristina. max was furious about all kir's situation and he was definitely not in a situation to think with him about a solution.

"max why don't you go to your room and rest for a bit" i told him.

I'm not gonna lie I'm worried about him max's heart is not so tough he has heart problems since he was a kid but that didn't stop him from being one of my most important men in the mafia he is awesome with chemicals.

"i don't want to rest so why don't you just tell me where the fuck were your mind when you told him that the wedding is tomorrow! You are selling her to him. Don't you know kir? He is going to fucking destroy her" he yelled "ENOUGH" i yelled back why does people think that when they yell they will make others listen "out. ORA" i said (now)He left the office while slamming the door and cursing kir and absolutely me.

"what are you going to do? You are definitely not giving her to him so what is the plan" Kristina said slowly. "you won't belive me but i don't have any" I said. I really don't. "so let's think about one because I'm not giving her to him" she said sitting on the chair infront of my office.*end of flashback*

That day Kristina came with that idea. I wasn't sure about it but i didn't have another so i agreed. My heart was breaking for everytime she looked at me trying to tell me what he is going to do to her and my telling her i don't care. And today when we were eating she was saying goodbye to us but without us knowing. Hearing her whisper i will miss you to arma and max made my hurt ache for not telling her that i won't sell her. But i couldn't. and now I'm standing in my office with loria behind me and Kristina just across from me arma and max are beside me just a few steps away and kir and his stupid brother infront of me.

"how many times i will have to tell you that i don't threat?i just do" I told Kar taking a step forward and immediately feeling coldness on my back for losing connect with her warm body "that's another threat" kar said "how about i show you?" i said looking at him he took a step forward i know he won't do anything he is not as brave as he want us to see him.

After some minutes with useless talk I sensed loria's hand on my back but not all of it because i was away from her just her fingers were on my back. I took a step back to help her holding into my back. She rested her hand on my back and i felt the warmth of her again.

"okay. I will take whoever this is but you better think about your plan from now because i will be done with this one soon" kır said. I was about to answer him when i heared her finally out of her silence.

"you won't take her" loria said with so much calm tone like she is the higher hand here. She isn't but she seems like she is.

"excuse me?" kir asked i turned to look at her earning coldness because she removed her hand "you heared me but i will say it again focus on my mouth you... will... not.. take... Her" she said. What is she even thinking about i don't think that she has any plan "and who will stop me? I have a contract" kir said.

She moved from behind me taking confident steps towards the table that the contract lays on. and i already know what her plan is.

Yeah exactly. She just took the paper and cut it into a hundred piece. And that's the truth she even counted every piece she cut off from the paper "so good luck now at finding the lora's name you won't be able to find even the L in lora" she said stepping on the now shattered paper.

I can't help it I'm proud. She was a minute before standing behind me in fear and now she just made kir angry everyone can see his face turning to red.

"i can take you instead" he said with not so calming tone "maybe you can try. But taking me! Nah i don't think so" she said. And yes she was right he can't take her because that will make a war between us and them and we will surely win maybe kir is dangerous but the Americans aren't.

He took a step towards her she seems like her mind is drifting because she wasn't looking at his eyes she was looking at the mirror behind him that shows him, her and Kristina behind her standing by the door.

"not so tough now are you?" he teased her smirking. Her hands were now on her head like she is protecting it but from what? "what happened? Did you already knew your mistake" kir asked agian his smirk go wider something is wrong. She looked at Kristina from the mirror and then she went to her shoving her away from the door in time so that the bullet is now in kir's heart.

Wait where did that bullet come from?

Chapter 20

K ai pov

I was standing still in my place loria was on the floor her hands on her head, Kristina beside her beginning to stand up, kir is on the floor, kar is in his place with a smile on his face, Arma on his way to help loria stand up, max looking at the hole that the bullet made.

"what the fuck? Where does this bullet came from?" Kristina said now pacing through the office i looked at arma and loria. Loria was now standing beside arma leaning against him trying to regain balance and i wasn't thinking about anything but her in his arms.

"kai focus on me God dammit" Kristina cursed. I looked at her "where does this bullet came from? And how did you find out and moved me away from the door? " she turned to loria asking her. She is not trusting her.

"this bullet came from...." she wince holding her head and i saw blood running from her nose.

I took a few steps towards her and took a tissue from the tissue box on my office's table. Her eyes were still closed i moved closer and put the tissue on her nose she didn't open her eyes but she leaned into my touch.

"arma take her to her room to rest, you too lora" i said because kar is still with us i don't want him to know about Kristina YET. "no no I'm fine you have to listen to what i have to say" loria said moving from arma's hands i rested on my office's table looking at her "the bullet came from someone i couldn't see his face but his eyes were green i managed to see it from his mask. Kir made him do that but he didn't know that i knew because it wasn't his mind where i knew this info from" she said looking at kar and we immediately understood. "okay loria now go to your room and take some rest" i told her.

Few moments later

I was still at my office while kar explained why he did that and all his trauma with his brother but what made me furious was these sentences "i was supposed to marry loria. I was the one who was going to fuck her. But he wanted her". They were fighting over who is going to fuck her?

"look kar we don't want to listen to all of this but i will make you a favor and tell you who is the only one that will fuck her *me*" i told him then dismissed him. Why i didn't kill him? Well I'm not in the mood. if i ever wanted to i will it's easy he is so helpless and weak that anyone can finish him.

I was now standing beside her bed looking down at her she looks so tired.

"dude staring is rude" she said while opening her eyes. I won't ask how she knew i was here because that will be stupid so instead i just choose to tease her "nah i don't think so" i said not leaving my place nor looking away from her face "is Kristina alright?" she asked. Wow isn't she adorable she is asking about someone that was yelling at her and not trusting her. "yeah. Are you?" i asked "yeah" she said standing up from the bed and walking towards the bathroom. I held her wrist stopping her she winces and i dropped it immediately.

"are you hurt?" i asked examining her wrist without asking for permission "yeah just that kir dude's hands were rough" she said. I found her wrist red and bruised is that from just grapping her? "yes it is, my body bruises easily" she said. agian I'm not asking how she knew because i let her in this time "prepare yourself we are going shopping" i said leaving her wrist "shopping?" she asked "yeah, I'm done with you wearing my clothes" i said. She blushed"okay i will be done in 15 minutes" she said pulling away and going into the bathroom.

Loria pov

I was in the car with kai driving I'm surprised that he is the one who is driving i thought that he will just make someone drive. We were headed to shopping. from where? i don't know and i didn't ask. i don't think it would be a good idea to even start a talk with him I'm still not over all of kir's situation and him not telling me about his plan.

"you are not talking?" he asked "yeah" i responded "and why is that?" he asked again opening a discussion with me. "because I'm not over you not telling me about all the Kristina thing. You let me think that you will sell me to him. You even made me say.." i stopped. No i don't want him to know that i was saying goodbye. He looked at me and then to the road.

"i made you say goodbye" he continued my sentence.

He heard me. He knew that i was in pain.

I looked at him and then i looked to the road again.

"it's not something to be ashamed of. I know someone that never do anything without saying goodbye first. Incase anything happened." he told me.

Afew minutes later.

"we are here" he said.

i opened the passenger door to find him standing here giving me his hand to help me out of the car how did he came here that fast?

"i can get out by myself you know" i said getting out from the car not taking his hand his hands fell beside him and as i was about to enter the mall infront of me he holds my hand yeah hand not my wrist he has avoided to touch my wrist since he saw it was bruised i know it is not something dangerous it's just my skin.

"there are some rules before we enter the mall loria" he said

Of course there are is there anything around him that don't have rules? "and those rules are?" i asked him "easy. You are not to talk to anyone,you are not to leave my side and you are not to raise your voice at me at any circumstances" he said his face turning serious he let me in his mind to show me that he is not bluffing or joking these rules are important to follow "okay" i accepted not like I was going to do any of them anyway.

We entered the mall and i felt his hand on my back leading me to where to go he was behind me but i couldn't feel any safer. We went to a few shops to buy what is needed.

Wow this dress is amazing on me. i don't know why but he made me buy so much clothes from every model. And he insisted on going in this final shop and then we will go. Now I'm wearing a red satan dress that reaches just my mid thight with strapes just from the back i look good in it.

"you haven't finished yet?" he asked.

Yeah he didn't let me buy anything before he sees it on me he has refused many dresses saying that it didn't fit me but i know that it's a lie he is just jealous.

"coming" i told him opening the curtains of the fitting room to see him sitting on the sofa infront of the fitting room his eyes were on his phone. I cleared my throat to tell him that I'm out he looked up from his phone and saw me. I could feel his eyes checking me out. Dude just control your eyes. I know for sure that i will be blushing by now because of his eyes checking me out.

"you done checking me out?" i asked him trying to take a hold of myself "nah not yet" he said his eyes roaming over my body "I'm not buying that" I said going in the fitting agian to start changing my clothes into his but i didn't get a chance as i feel hot breath behind me "what the hell kai? Out now" i told him trying to make him go but i couldn't move him "you look pretty" he told me with lust in his eyes "thanks!" i said "now if you don't mind i want to get rid of this dress" i said innocently "if you wanted to get rid of it all you have to do is asking" he said moving closer to me i felt gousebumbs all over my skin "ehm, kai you should go" i told him he closed his eyes and moved closer to me then he kissed me and I wasn't complaining.

his lips were soft he gave me a slow kiss filled with warmth and all i could do is kissing him back. Well trying to kiss him back this was my second kiss after all and i wasn't kissing back at the first one. I was so lost in this feeling i feel like i can stay like this forever. His kiss turned to a passionate one with his hands on my waist making me go closer to him.

"ehm ehm" we heared someone clears her throat. Kai groans while turning to the woman behind him. The woman looked to him and then she apologized and went away he turned to me and now i could see why she ran away. I'm sure my cheeks are red by now he smiled then took my hand and went out from the shop and to the car.

"how about we continue our business?" he said smirking at me. I didn't look at him. i can't. i just looked outside "well we will have to continue it later then" he said while turning my head to give a quick kiss then we drove to the house back.

Chapter 21

Loria pov

We were on our way to the house. I'm still in that dress he didn't even let me change he just moved me to the car so fast. What surprised me was the man on the cashier not even asking for the dress's price. It wasn't cheap so why he didn't talk about it he just looked at us then looked down at what he was doing.

"what are you thinking about?" he asked not moving his eyes from the road "that man didn't ask you about the dress's price also it's not a little" i told him "maybe i own the mall" he told me. He owns it? Yes I didn't see him giving them money or anything but i thought that he already dealt with it while i was changing. He smiled okay now i really want to know what's on his mind why don't he let me in?

"your nose is bleeding again" he told me giving me a tissue "thanks" i told him taking it from his hand and putting it on my nose. And He didn't say any other word to me.

I heared his phone ringing he answered it putting it on speaker. Wow he trusts me to listen to his calls.

"yes arma" he answered "yes to you boss you called me" arma said confused "yeah call the doctor and tell him to be in the house in 15 minutes max not one minute late" he told him "what happened? Has anything happened to loria?" arma asked i saw kai holding the wheel tight his knuckles turns white "just do what i fuckin told you" he told him then hanged up.

"ehm" i cleared my throat "what?" he asked me firmly "can you just pull off to any restaurant?" i asked him "why?" he asked me back "so that i can change" i told him.

He looked down at me realizing that I'm still wearing that dress he released a slow fuck then he speed up the car. I don't mind though i love fast driving.

He put his leg at the brakes so fast that i almost hit my head if it wasn't for his hands on me holding me back. Yeah i wasn't wearing my seat belt. What a foolish thing to do when kai is driving.

"you okay?" he asked me i looked at him his head was bruised means that he also wasn't wearing his seat belt and that he didn't use his hands to stop himself from the Hit.

"kai your head" i told him. He looked at himself in the mirror but he just shaked his head telling me that he is okay. And that we are here. I looked around to see that there is a small restaurant on my right. "okay i will be here in a minute" i told him opening the door but he held my hand and went to the back of the car to give me some clothes of his.

"i thought you were done with me wearing your clothes!" i teased him. He smirked "yeah and now I'm thinking about starting to just take them off" he said i started blushing and then went out of the car hearing him laughing loudly. FOR THE FIRST TIME I GUESS.

Kai pov

My jealousy was just making me not able to see anything but her and arma laughing loudly as they are used to, him putting his hands on her and her just moves closer to him and then I saw a restaurant i pulled the brakes so fast that she was about to hit her head if it wasn't for my hands on her holding her back resulting for me to get the hit. Guess i deserve it.

"are you okay?" i asked her so worried about her so worried that i will be like my father and hurting a woman she was looking at me with worried expression "kai you head!" she told me i looked at me head at the mirror only to find it a little bruised i shaked my head to tell her that I'm fine. I wanted to tell her that I'm okay because she is. How? I don't know. Why? I don't know either.

"okay i will be here in a minute" i heared her voice taking me out of my thinking. I held her hands giving her some clothes of mine that i always keep on my car in case i needed to change "i thought you were done with me wearing your clothes!" she said looking at the clothes in her hands then to me. So she doesn't forgets easily and she just focuses on every thing.I smirked thinking that she is so smart i really wanted to meet someone like her for ages "yeah and now I'm thinking about starting to just take them off" i teased her.

She is red as tomatoes right now looking anywhere but my eyes and then she was out of the car.

After a few moments i saw her getting out from the restaurant with the sweat pants that i gave her in her hands and that amazing red dress she was just wearing the T-shirt. Fuck she looks so fuckable right now. Control yourself kai. I was so turned on by just looking at her and then I saw some guy looking at her with not so innocent look and all of my emotions turned into anger i took a pic of the guy before she enters the car.

"didn't you forget something?" i told her clenching my Jaw she looked at me not understanding. I took the sweatpants of her hands showing her what she forgot "it is so big i couldn't fit" she said with softness and innocent in her figures. She don't know what she is doing to me right now. I put my leg on the gas and drove back to the house.

We were on the gate she was preparing herself to get out "you won't move from the car i will go in and out in 5 minutes stay still in the car" i told her. She looked at me confused "why?" she asked i didn't answer.

I got out from the car locking it behind me i saw disbelief and betrayal in her eyes. It's not you that i don't trust you love it's my men. Not like i don't trust them at all i just don't trust all of my men around her only a few so this locking thing is for them not you. I hope she read my mind so that she knows that i do trust her.

In 3 minutes i was infront of the car opening it and going to the driver seat again giving her some shorts of mine "wear those" I told her and to my surprise she did without even asking.

We went out from the car and into the house and she went straight to her room. She is hurt about what i did means that she didn't read my mind. I will go to her later i have some work to attend now.

I walked to my office and called for arma, max and Nik "so how is the project going on?" i asked i know that arma is the only one who is going to answer "not so good" he told me "her mother again ?" i asked him "yes" he told me "nik you are going to abria prepare yourself" i told him actually it's a punishment i haven't punished him about what he did to loria yet "what?" he asked "I'm not going in that stupid project. I have a life here" he told me "yes you have and you will be here after you do your job in abria" i told him "no kai I'm not going send max" he told me "YOU ARE GOING" i told him with a demanding tone he just looked at me then went outside.

"max do what we talked about and tell me when it's done" i told him too and dismissed him now it's arma's turn. Arma is like my brother for so many years he is my third brother but i don't like the connection that he has with loria "now to you Arma i have to ask you what feelings do you have for loria?" i asked him "what do you mean?" he asked "you heared me" i told him agian leaning back in my chair looking at his eyes "nothing. Loria just needs friends and I'm helping her with that I'm just trying to make her feel home" he told me and i don't need loria's mind reading thing to know that he is saying the truth "okay arma. Now tell me about what the Russians did agian" i told him.

I was in my office for hours now working on the Russians problems, abria's problem and some other things that i arrange to my business but i felt so hungry and i think no one is up now it's 3 in the morning so i decided that I will make myself a sandwich. I went to the kitchen only to find her *again* she was wearing a sports pants and my T-shirt it is so big on her she looks adorable. She was cooking. How could she eat all this food and still be in a fuckin good shape! All the girls that i knew are just eating healthy food and lots of them don't even eat in front of anyone but not her she eats whatever she want whenever she want and in front of anyone.

"you have to stop that hobby of yours" she said "what hobby?" i asked her leaning on the wall in the entrance if the kitchen "the hobby of you going in and not making any sound" she said. Okay so if I'm not doing any sound how she finds out that I'm here every time? "i will make sure the next time i go in you will be the one to make a sound" i looked at her smirking. She didn't understand. She just looked at me confused and went to continue what she was doing.

"so what are you cooking now?" i asked sitting on a chair "I'm cooking some rice and sweet and sour chicken" she told me "you want some?" she continued "sure" i told her.

She was moving in the kitchen so fast not missing any ingredients not doing anything wrong she is an amazing cook.

"I'm done" she told me putting a plate in front of me with rice and some chicken and then she got herself one and sat beside me. I took a spoon and my mouth watered it tastes so good "it's so good" i told her "thanks" she told me knowing that it is. she is just so confident of her cooking skills we finished eating and she was having a sauce beside her mouth i looked at her then leaned in removing the sauce from her mouth then liking my finger "ew dude you could have told me or just used a tissue inste.." she was cut be my mouth on hers she has an amazing soft lips i kissed her a soft small kiss not thinking about turning it to any other kind.

"oh my god i knew that you were going to be a couple" arma said walking in she broke the kiss fast and her cheeks turned red i was still in my place smirking "ehm i should leave you two" she said walking past me but i held her hand moving her closer to me "okay love birds i understood the assignment" arma said leaving the kitchen i turned her to face me "so you broke our kiss" i told her with a hurt expression on my face her hands moved to my chest supporting her stand "so how about we start again?" i told her leaning in to kiss her again.

Chapter 22

Loria pov

"i don't know how you didn't tell me! I'm your friend" arma said pouting.

He was so sad that i didn't tell him that me and kai were together *we aren't but he is sure that we are* he saw us a few days ago kissing in the kitchen and since that day he is sure that we are together and hiding it from him. I don't know if we are why would we hide it? And especially why from him! Kai didn't even speak with me since then and i didn't see him either. He was always at his office working or not in the house at all like now he was at some company of his.I'm sitting here in the kitchen with arma having lunch and he is not stopping.

"arma i told you hundreds of times we are not together. Why are you so sure that we are?" i asked him. "are you really asking this question?" he tilted his head looking at me confused "yes, okay we kissed so what? I don't think that it was his first kiss" i said

I'm trying to not make a big deal out of it but to me *it is* I'm only had a few kisses and it's from him i didn't kiss any other man and i was mad because of that i Don't want him to think that he is special.

"it isn't but it is for you" arma continued. "you are not going to shut up are you?" i asked him holding me head between my hands "no" he told me smirking "okay so can we make a deal!" i said "what deal?" he asked me confused. I straightened at my chair "i will prove you that this kiss means nothing and you will stop Bother me" i told him "okay but how!" he asked smiling. Something i learned about arma he loves games "by kissing other man" i told him. He was shocked by what i said okay me too but i have to prove that this kiss meant nothing although it didn't mean nothing *they don't need to know this* "deal?" i asked "with one condition" he told me smiling "and what is that?" i asked "I'm the one who is going to tell you whom" he said smirking "deal" i said without thinking it won't be that hard would it! "so who am i going to kiss?" I asked him "nik" he said pointing to nik who was now entering the kitchen. Okay maybe i should have thought more "okay" i told him

Where was my fucking my mind when i accepted that challenge. Just to prove that I'm not with kai i will have to kiss that fucker. Arma made a very hard choice i mean dude that man harassed me and now I'm going to go to him and kiss him and then explaining to him that it meant nothing. Okay loria you can do that

I was going in the living room arma and nik are sitting one is on the couch and the other is leaning on the wall i moved to the couch sat on it and looked at the big TV screen that plays iron man 2 nik was beside me watching the film i closed my eye and moved fast and pressed my lips on his a fast kiss with no emotions and then i moved away from him opening my eyes i saw kai standing at the entrance of the living room.

Like man in all those days i didn't see you and now you are standing here at the same place that i and nik kissed. Karma is a bitch

Kai pov

What the fuck!! Why on earth has she done that? I looked at her. Her cheeks are red with embarrassment her eyes were on the floor. Nik beside her is clueless what was that for he don't mind being kissed he is just confused and arma beside me is looking at me with a smirk on his face that i will wipe it off when i catch him alone

I moved towards her grapped her hand and went to my bedroom yeah not my office. There are people in my office that's why I came today early. I have a meeting with some people finishing some business.

I shoved her into the room and closed the door behind me she fell to the floor i looked at her letting her into my mind to see that I'm furious to make her fear me

Why you did that? Did you forgot that this was nik? The one the harassed you? Are you that hopeless?

"no" i heared her "I'm not hopeless and i didn't forget. It was just a game between me and arma" she told me getting up from the floor "a game? The girl that just got her first kiss afew weeks ago! She is playing now? What are you planning to be a Hooker or something?" i bursted with anger. Her face turned blank she couldn't answer any of my questions. I was do mad at her she kissed my fucking brother for God's sake

She tried to move past me to open the door key word *tried* i held her by her waist her head is leaning onto my chest tightening my grip at her "let go of m-me" she told me taking a breath in "i won't. I will never let go of you i will just hold you like that" i told her "k-kai l-let go of m-me" she said again talking slowly "no" i told her moving my head to rest on her shoulder "kai i-i can't brea-ath" she said her heart starts beating faster

i loosened my grip on her she moved away from me catching her breath

"are you okay?" i asked her moving closer to her. She sat on the floor "i can't breath in the Narrow spaces" she told me ."why?" i asked. "I don't know i just can't" she told me "I'm sorry i didn't know" i told her "i only did it because arma was pushing me. Telling me that we are a couple. I was just trying to get him off of me by proving that our kiss meant nothing" she told me. I will have to have a talk with arma "you don't have to prove anything to anyone. You could have just told me. And i have to tell you that. that kiss meant something. i like you so much loria i can't imagine someone touching you in a wrong way, hurting you nor even looking at you a disrespectful look " i told her and that's the truth i really like her so much."thank you for letting me in" she told me "that wasn't on purpose" i told her again smiling and leaning towards her giving her a slow gentle kiss showing her that i really mean what i said.

Chapter 23

K ai pov

I was at my office having a meeting with some of the Americans after i dealt with my other business meeting and dealt with loria i didn't deal with arma yet but i surely will after I'm done with this meeting

"so you are telling me that you want a shipment of mine as Compensation for the death of kir!" i said they are mad if they think that i will accept that "yes" bruly said. Bruly is the Americans mafia boss he is also my Uncle my mother and him were so good with each other but after they gave her to my father they stopped talking he didn't want to have anything with her.

"and who told you that i will accept that?" i said "me" he told me again arma chuckled behind me earning a glare from bruly "i don't see anything to laugh about" bruly said again

"forgive me that was my doing" loria said emerging behind him we didn't see her coming in and i don't think that's why Arma chuckled "and you are?" bruly said "I'm loria" she said her head high looking at him "i think that you will have to rethink about your compensation because what you want is impossible" i told him making him turn to me again but i was looking at loria behind him (what are you doing here?) she smiled at me to let me know that she read my mind "and why is that?" bruly said.

"i can tell you why" she said making him turn to look at her again "because we are not the ones who killed him it was his work against him. My mother always told me a sentence in Arabic that explains this situation" she said " "
she continued

"what do you mean?" he asked her "i mean that he Paid a spy to kill someone but i knew and somehow he was the one that the bullet laid in" she explained leaving out some details

"so you are the supernatural girl!" he asked amazed by her "yup, That's me" she said walking and standing beside me "so as you heared bruly your compensation is refused you can now move to your place" i said

"so what about other deal?" bruly said "we are listening" i said. i saw loria smile from the corner of my eyes without knowing the reason but I'm glad

"how about buying something from you?" he told me "and what is that thing?" i asked. He glanced at loria and smirked "your deal is declined" i told him with a serious expression "why?" he told me "you didn't even listened to what i have to say" he continued

"but i know what is that thing and i also know what he refused and i can reassure you that it's the samething" loria said from beside me with a serious expression that matches mine.

"okay" he said standing up closing his suit jacket's button "we will see each other soon" he said smirking and holding his hands to loria to shake she looked at his hands "Non credo. Ciao bruly" she said looking at him not shaking his hands. I smiled and waved him "bye bruly" i said smirking (i don't think so. Bye bruly)

He stormed out of the office. As soon as the door closed i found Arma laughing "that was so good" he said turning to loria highfiveing her. I looked at him

"now to you Arma" i said turning the chair to him. He looked at me and as soon as he saw my expression he went to the door but max closed the door "dude are you with him?" arma asked "he is my brother after all" max said smiling

I stood up from the chair with loria behind me and went to him "so arma you know what I'm going to do right?" i asked him with a smirk on my face "actually i have no idea but i don't think it's a good thing" he said "yup that's right" loria said looking at the floor

"loria I'm your friend" arma looked at loria "yes you are" she said "so you are leaving me to him?" he asked her again "i don't think that i have anything to do in that matter. I'm his bodyguard afterall" she said smiling

"so you were bothering her about something that you saw. Am i right?" i asked him "what? I was bothering her? She is my friend i could never do that" he told me nervously. Loria chuckled at him "i don't think that you are so convincing" she told him. "Παιδιά, είμαι φίλος σας." he said (guys I'm your friend) i laughed at him "okay arma we know that you are our friend but you Will pay for what you did" I told him "okay but what is the payment" arma asked "a boxing match" i said "ouch. I think you are going to hell" max said arma sighted "i don't think That i have a choice" arma surrendered. "tomorrow 9 am at the gym" i said leaving the office hearing loria screaming from laughter at the office.

Loria pov

"stopppp" i said laughing so loud arma was on me tickling me because i didn't stop kai from doing this punishment to him "m..ax" i begged him to help me but he was still laughing at me and arma "no one is going to help you" arma said continuing tickling me "what is happening here? " nik said entering the office. Arma stopped "nothing" he told him giving me his hand i took it and stood up "i don't think that the office is somewhere to play in" he said "yes we know take it easy man" max said "i don't think that this would be the way to talk to kai when he know about that" he said leaving the office.

I looked at arma and max and started laughing out loud they joined me and we were on the floor dying from laughter

"i don't know why he is like that? He don't seem like your brother at all" i told max "yeah many people told us" he said "don't think that you are saved come here" arma said i ran outside the office arma behind meAnd as soon as i got out from the office i ran into some girl she was holding her phone and her phone fell from her hand "ow. Watch where you are going" the girl yelled at me "sorry" i told her smiling "what are you smiling about? you seeing a clown in front of you?" she told me

i looked at her she has a black hair, a model body and a full makeup face " "   i whispered "excuse me" she said "oh nothing sorry i was just running to somewhere" i said

"come here" arma said coming behind me "oh arma so you are arma's bitch" she said smirking. Arma looked at her with a bored expression on his face "landa" he said "nice to meet you too" she said "you finally found yourself a bitch" she continued I'm so mad right now that i can burn her from just eye sight "you are?" i asked her "landa" she said "yeah i know that your name is landa arma already mentioned it. I'm asking landa who" i asked again "she had a one night stand with kai and she is after him since then" arma explained "rude" she said

Yeah how cliché i think that i know how our relationship will be "okay so let's get to the point from now he doesn't want you so you will have to stop coming here so let's skip all those cliché situations about you trying to do things to make me upset or make me leave or all these things. am i making myself clear?" i told her (what the fuck? How this bitch is talking to me like that!)."to save us all the situation when you are the devil Barbie bitch and I'm the little innocent dear. I can reassure you that I'm not innocent at all" i told her and took a step towards her "am i making myself clear?" i told her she didn't answer "good" i told her and went to my room and i could hear arma's thought behind me (wow

I'm impressed. Congrats no one ever made her quite like this before) i smiled and started to walk up the stairs

Late at night

I opened my eyes at the voices of someone yelling i pulled the sheets off of me and opened the door i could hear landa yelling "you can't refuse me I'm landa. You can't make me a one night stands of yours I'm not your whore" she was yelling i went to where the voices came from and i found myself outside kai's room with him standing there his hands in his pockets he was wearing a grey sweatpants and a black T shirt he was looking at her with bored expression (just stop yelling woman) i heared his mind.

His eyes went to me i was wearing only a T-shirt and not any T-shirt.

It was his T-shirt i don't know why but his T shirts are so comfortable.

He was looking at me not caring about landa i heared what she was thinking about and i went straight to him he was confused i stood in front of him and held her hands that were going to land on his face

"tsk tsk tsk that's rude" i told her. She pulled her hand from my hold and pushed me backwards only to hit kai's chest he held me his hands on my waist

"oh that's why you told me about all the Barbie situation. That's what you meant by i making you upset or leave. You are his new fuck doll" she laughed and i could feel him getting angry behind me

"something like that" i told her "do you think that he will treat you better?" she asked laughing "he is just going to fuck you and then you will be like all of us" she continued "nah, you are a whore. I'm a soldier" i said smiling at her "we will see what you are in the end of the day" she looked at me then at him.

He grapped me to give me a soft kiss in front of her. For the first time i felt disappointed at him disappointed at me for hurting another woman's feeling. I broke the kiss not looking at his eyes and looked at her to find her trying so hard to hold her tears i looked at the floor embarrassed of what i did to her

He held my waist,put me behind him and was now facing her

"i think our answer is clear now" he said i could hear her mind she was so sad she wanted to cry so hard but she was a strong woman she didn't give him the satisfaction of seeing her crying

"just wait until that get to my father" she told him. Then she went down

He turned to me with a smile on his face and his eyes on my waist "so what about we continue what we were doing" he said smirking and leaning down towards me i turned my face.

He looked at me confused "what is wrong?" he asked me i took a step back from him "don't ever do that again i will not be used against other womans to hurt them because they didn't know that you were doing a one night stand " i told him and stormed to my room closing it behind me.

Chapter 24

Kai povl was at the gym waiting for her she walked in wearing sports bra and leggings "what was that you did yesterday?" i asked her i couldn't stop thinking about it. I thought that she will be angry about landa but she wasn't. She was angry with me.

"what?" she asked looking at me "you know what I'm talking about" i told her "yes" she said "so?" i asked again i want to know why she did that. "i did that because i will not hurt any other woman's emotions kai. You didn't read her mind. you didn't know what she felt. She is a tough person she kept her tears she didn't give you the satisfaction. She just refused to let you step on her and you didn't give a shit you just smashed her with kissing me infront of her" she exploded.

Wow i didn't think that she will be like that about her i thought that she will hate her i was even thinking of what to tell her to make her realize that I don't care about landa but that's not the problem the problem is That she hurt landa's feelings "can we skip this and go straight to the training" she told me "yes" i told her. She was taking the boxing gloves but i took it from her "not today" i told her "so what are we doing today?" she asked. "fitness and gun shot" i told her and We began our fitness exercises.

I was worried when we finished she wasn't so good at the fitness exercises she actually hate it especially the weight lifting she was on the floor catching her breath

"are we done yet?" she asked "yes we are" i said "go to your room take a shower and change then meet me at the field" i told her going out from the gym "where is that field?" she asked "ask max to bring you" i told her and went to my room.

I'm seriously so confused about her i have feeling for her i don't like her being mad at me. I don't know what I'm going to do about landa's problem. I opened the cold water and stepped into the shower. There is also abria's problem i haven't solved yet. nik didn't go there yet my mom refused to let him go there and i need max here beside me i don't know who to send back there but i will have to do something.

I was at the field with loria she was standing in front of me holding the gun aiming it to the target there is no one but us here today i made sure of that i took a step towards her correcting her hold on the gun

"stay still. Take a breath in and dont let it out until you shoot" i instructed her she did what i said and fired. it landed in the middle of the target

"that's good" i told her taking a step back letting her shoot the next one and she shot it without blinking landing on the middle of the target again "you are good at aiming" i told her "now take some steps back" i continued putting my hands on her waist "i can wake on my own" she told me but i refused to drop my hands i instructed her again to where to stand. "now try to shoot two bullets one in the heart and the other in the head" i told her. She took a breath shooting but she missed the heart it landed in his chest "not bad" i told her "again" i continued.

After an hour and a half

"you are good but you just need to focus" i told her she let a breath out "next time we will try on the sides" i told her she nodded and put the gun down and moved past me "just one mistake" i told her taking the gun out

"you forget to put the safety back on" i said aiming it to her "two things you never forget. One is to never let your safety off after you finish shooting" i told her "and the other" she said moving towards me she seems so sure that i will not shoot

"to never underestimate the one holds the gun" i said shooting right beside her shoulder the bullet just went up-side her shoulder and scratched her.

She flinched but didn't move. I put the safety back on and went to her she looked at me

"okay" she said turning her back to me and moving to the house but i grapped her hand and turned her to face me. Our lips were almost touching she looked at my eyes

"you good?" i asked "what do you see?" she told me. I wasn't asking about her shoulder i know that it's nothing it won't even leave a scar i know that. I was asking about her not her shoulder "i can't see anything you hide your emotions well" i told her and i wasn't lying she is really good at it "I'm not" she told me. I know that she isn't but i don't know what to do to make her good to make her see me again as she was seeing me now she is just seeing me as kai lionail the bad boy who uses women as a one nightstand.

"kai there is a problem" arma said running towards me loria took a step back "what now arma?" i asked him "abria" he told me and that word was enough to make me go to the office hurriedly.

I opened my office's door to find max there "what happened" i asked him "nik" he told me "Che cazzo ha fatto ora?" i said slamming my hand on the office's walls (What the fuck he did now?)

"he told loria's mother that she is dead and that it was the city that did that so they refused to work and even worse they began to make damages in abria" he told me

My fucking brother. He is damaging my project *our project* out of anger and selfishness "get him out" i told them "we can't. they captured him" arma explained "who did?" i asked "loria's mother" max said looking at the floor.

"send me to her" i heared her from behind me "what?" arma asked "you heared me arma send me there" she said. I looked at her. No i can't lose her. Think kai there must be another solution. You are the fucking smart one you have to think.

"but the x rays" arma said "i don't care. I have to send nik back to his home" she said. She is thinking about nik even after he harassed her after he mistreated her after a lot of bad things that he have done to her. "get a source of power" i told arma "but kai.." "do what i say. I have an idea" i interrupted him.

He went to get a source of power "move" I told max he moved away from the project and the computer i sat on the chair, opened my computer and started working

A few hours later i was able to update the door to make it get less x rays so that it won't affect her so much

"I'm done" i told them loria looked at me i could sense her stress she didn't want to go back to abria but she is doing that to help us to solve my brother's problems

I looked at her with and noded my head to her i let her into my mind to know that i have so much feelings for her that i will not leave her there so much i will get her out as soon as possible ane then i blocked my mind again so that she won't be able to read my frightened thoughts. I was 98% sure that i will make her come here again but the other 2% are filled with fear of not seeing her again. She walked towards me and hugged me tightly i hugged her back not letting her go i don't want to. I hid my face into her nick smelling her scent like it would be the last time. i finally let her go

"focus on your breath and once you are with nik tell me" i told her. On the past days she learnt to control her powers more but i was counting on her new power that she will get once she is back in abria i made the x rays softer yes but i put some energy in it like it was in the door she broke when she came her only the useful one. She nodded her head and kissed me a soft kiss holds so much emotions "remind me to tell you something important when i come back" she told me smiling "what thing" i asked her "you will know when I'm back" she told me and kissed me one last time then we put the straps on her i looked at her one last time and then she was gone. Arma looked at me "did it work?" he asked "i don't know I'm with you in my fucking office" i told him then looked back at abria. She will make it. She is a tough girl she will make it work

3 days laterWe haven't heard anything from her nothing happened even the problems in abria wasn't solved i don't know what is that supposed to mean. Does that means that she didn't go there? Then where is she? I was at my office looking at abria i couldn't find anything about where she was the only thing that will make us know that she is there is that the problems will be solved but no problem was solved not even one. Nik was there still captured by them my mom was going mad i couldn't face her she kept on telling me that i was the one who sent him there and that I'm the reason for all of that. My father didn't give a shit he just keeps on agreeing that this project is bad and that i have to finish it.

I heared a knock on my office.

"Entra" i saidI saw Arma going inside the office "kai you have to get some sleep" he told me "no" i told him "kai she wouldn't want you to suffer like that" he told me. i don't need those fucking words. "arma save yourself all those words and advices i won't go out from here until i find her" i told him still working on my computer "her last words to me were about you" he told me sitting on the sofa his eyes on the floor. That's new i didn't know that she talked to him.

"when was that?" i asked him resting my back into the chair and looking at him "when you were doing the update on the door" he told me "what did she tell you?" I asked "she told me to take care of you. And that she loved you that would have been the thing that she will tell you when she comes back" he told me.

She loved me!

Chapter 25

I found myself in the woods. The woods are always a place to get lost. yeah cliché i know but what am i supposed to do? i found myself in the middle of the woods after i said goodbye to kai.

His stupid brother just got himself in trouble and i couldn't let him be in it i just had to do something. Kai told me that i will get new powers but i found non. I walked to the nearest house 'gru's family' mr and ms gru were so kind to everyone. Everyone in the city loved them not me though i happen to be the only one in the city that don't love them I'm just not a fan of there attitude but i have to go inside it's freezing out here

I knocked on their door and mr gru opened the door "hi mr gru. How are you!" i asked him putting on a fake smile "loria! Where were you Your mother was searching for you!" he asked me "yeah long story. Can you let me in please? it's freezing out here" i told him "yeah sure come on in" he told me

Their house were like ours there isn't much difference the only difference that their house in missing the modern touch considering that they don't have anyone young mr and ms gru were almost 65 years old but they were the perfect couple for each others they love the same things, their living style is the same and even their laugh is the same. They were black with brown eyes and white hair considering their age.

"hello dear." that was ms gru coming out from the kitchen "your mom was searching for you all over the city. Where have you been?" she asked me "it's a long story" i told them "i think you have a time to tell us" she told me again "i wish That i had but I'm just so tired. I promise you that i will in the morning it's just that i don't have any power left to talk" i lied i know that first thing that i will do in the morning is going out from their house and to mine to take nik and find a way to contact kai. "yeah sure darling you may sleep in the guest room i will show you the way" she said leading me upstairs. i opened the door to find a small bed, a window beside it and a bathroom "i will let you rest" she said closing the door behind her.

I throw myself on the bed, closed my eyes and started to use my power to see what is kai doing i found him in his office on his computer.. oh what i would do to just touch his pretty face

"oh loria what i did to you!" he said putting his hand on his face. No please don't tell me that you are blaming yourself.

"did you find her?" max asked him entering the office "not yet" he told him his eyes not leaving the computer "she must have been in somewhere there just search again" max told him "Max Fuori. Ora" he told him (max out. Now). Max looked at him and then he went out. Then it was all black. I think that is only what my powers allows me to see. Now i need some sleep

Next dayI opened my eyes to the sun entering the room from the window i went to the bathroom took a shower then i opened my room door sneaking out not making any sound the people in Abria wakes up early but not this couple they love their sleep they actually stay up till dawn watching the sun rise it's a habit for them.

I opened the door and went straight to our farm but there was no one here but worse our farm was damaged the soil was beginning to be damaged because it was rearly getting water. what happened here?

"mom" i called for her but there was no answer "grams" stil no answer. where are they? "loria" i heared someone from behind me "mr tren" i said looking at him.

That was our neighbor he was a friend of my father they were best buddies

"where were you?" he asked me "what happened here mr tren?" i asked him "your mother is no longer working here she left the farm since you were gone" he explained "where is she?" i asked him "I'm sorry but.. i Don't know" he said looking at the floor. I left him and ran to my house it is dark no one is in there i didn't want to come back here yes but i also didn't want all of that to happen "mom" i called for her but no one answered me "grams" still no answer i opened the door and went inside the house is so dark. I opened the curtains to let the light in but i only saw dust on the furniture they were covered with a white cover the dust is thick on it means that they were gone for a long time i sat on the floor looking at our living room it was filled with our sounds once. We were fighting yes but we were a family. I miss my family i miss our fights i miss them all i miss all those memories. I want them to be happy yes i love the city i just don't like the idea of being trapped her i closed my eyes remembering all our memories all of it even the fighting ones i started to feel my body goes limp and then also that i was asleep a few moments ago the sleep consumed me again.

I woke up to a sound in the backyard

"mom?" i called but again i got no answer i stood up walked to the backyard hurriedly only to find ne in our backyard.

Ne is the city's dog it has no owner. He just keep going every house in the city searching for food or a warm place to sleep "ne" i said and sat on the floor he ran to me "hey buddy" i said to him "you want some food?" i asked him and stood up going into the house with him following behind me

I opened the fridge to find something to eat i only found two cans of beans "well. I guess one is for you and one is for me" i told him opening the can of beans to put in front of him i hope he eats it i don't know if he will eat it but our fridge contains nothing else to eat. All of it are rotten only the can because her expired date was to another month.

I layed on the couch in the living room and closed my eyes to see kai again he was still in his office working on his computer with no one with him i missed him i missed his touch so much i really want to finish this fast so i can go back to him but how will i do that? My mother will never allow it. I will think about it when i see my mother right now i will just stay with kai.

The next dayI didn't sleep i already had my sleep twice a day i was just with kai in his office watching him with my powers i love him for the first time i love someone. He is my first everything and I'm glad about that. i want him to be my last too but right now i need to find nik and find a way to go back there.

I was on my way to the middle of the city. When people see me they will tell me anything about her or even telling my mother that I'm here.

I was there standing in the middle of the city but no one saw me so i had to do something to make them see me. I climbed to the ancient tree that were in the middle of the city and sat on a branch but i decided to look at what kai's first maybe for the last time i don't know how i will be busy these coming hours or maybe days

He was in his office still on his computer. Just leave the fucking computer kai. I found arma opening the office's room and they talked for a while but what made me angry was what arma told him. Why the hell would he tell him that I'm in love with him! I was supposed to be the one who tells him that important information but what surprised me even more what kai told him "she loves me? How? What would you feel if you loved someone? I have feelings for her a very strong ones but i don.." "kai you love her" arma interrupted him. He is not sure that he loves me and fucking arma told him that i love him. He doesn't feel the same. Fuck

I opened my eyes and yelled from the tree branch "heyy can you please look at me" i yelled to everyone "I'm loria" i continued "does anyone knows where my mom is??" i asked after gaining the people's attention "loria" i heared my mom's voice "mom" i said trying to know where her voice came from "I'm here baby" she told me.

I rushed downstairs to find her crying i ran to her arms

"i missed you" i told her "i missed you too baby. Where were you?" she asked me "are you alright?" she asked me again examining me "I'm fine mom" i told her "where is grams?" i asked "she is in the tent" she told me "tent? You left our home, Our farm to live in a tent?" i asked her taking a step away from her "i didn't want to do anything that the city made me do" she told me "mom the city didn't take me from you. I'm the one that left" i told her "what?" she asked me "yes mom i left i wanted my freedom" i told her " "

        i continued "you are the one who told me that" i said

"but.." she started "no buts mom i need my freedom you can't lose your life because i wanted my freedom. You can't leave our farm to be damaged like that. You can't leave ne. He was outside our home yesterday searching for us for the warmth that we always gave him. You can't let all of that because i left "i told her

."i just came here for something and i wil leave again" i continued" and what Is that thing?" she asked me."someone actually. I'm here for the man you captured" i told her "okay" she told me "take her to him" she said. And a strange looking man came to me holding ny shoulder and leading me away.

"where are you taking me?" i asked him "mom?" i looked at her she wasn't looking at me "hey you are hurting my shoulder let go of me" i told the man again but he did nothing he was like a deaf person not answering anything not doing any reaction to what I'm saying he just kept dragging me into the woods.

He let go of me once we were outside a cave "he is inside" he told me. "so you have a tongue" i told him but he didn't answer me he just turned his back to me and walked away.

I walked inside the cave to find mr pri and mr lo guarding a prison i didn't know that it was here in the first place i only knew that this place was not a good place to go around. why? i didn't know.

"loria" mr pri said "what are you doing her?" he asked me "i came here to see the man who told you that i was gone" i told him "does your mom knows that you are here?" mr lo asked me "actually she is the one who sent me to see him" i told him.He opened a door leading to some room a step inside and the door closed behind me "nik" i called for him "here" he said pointing his hand up "okay I'm with you. now we need to get out of here" i was thinking out loud "how?" he asked me laughing at me "like you came in!" i told him angrily. I want to slap him so hard but I'm afraid of the consequences. I'm alone with him after all "there is no way out of here" he said again "dude just shut the fuck up" i told him "feisty i like it" i heared some voice coming out from a dark corner "who is there?" i asked taking a step towards him "on one special" the voice told me "okay 'no one special' why are you here?" i asked him "you think you are funny? " he said coming out from the shadows and i found a white muscled man with brown hair and brown eyes

"loria meet gab. He is the punisher here" nik told me "i did nothing to be punished" i said "we will see about that" gab said and went straight towards me delivering a punch to my rips and i went to the floor.

"i wasn't prepared to being beaten yet" i told him sarcastically "you think that it's a good time to make us see your sense of humor?" nik said coming towards me trying to make me stand but gab took his hand and threw him towards the wall. "who told you to help her?" he asked him "no one" nik said "so why making yourself a hero?" gab said delivering a kick to nik's back.

Nik didn't respond to him so he turned his back to him and his face to me "so why did they put you here in the first place? Why they want to punish you?" he asked me "no idea man" i said he was about to deliver a kick to my rips but i held his leg remembering kai's training and trapped him on the floor with my legs around his neck "so now. Will you tell me why they put you here?" i asked him sarcastically i know that he won't answer because he wasn't able to breath

"what the cat got your tounge?" i asked again "i don't think that you making him angry will make it better" nik said with a shaky voice beside me "relax i have it under con.." i wasn't able to finish my sentence because in a minute he was standing with me still around his neck slamming me into the walls i went to the floor on my rips after like 5 slams into the wall

"ow" i whimpered "not so tough now are you?" gab said sarcastically. Using my own sarcasm against me. Yeah karma Is a bitch. He kicked me in my rips one more time before mr lo inject him with something

"are you alright?" he asked us "yeah" nik said i was on the floor my mind was beginning to drift and then i saw kai in his office but this time he was like he sensed me "loria?" he called for me "I'm with him" i said and then everything went black.

Chapter 26

K ai pov

"Loria?" i said feeling her presence in the office with me "I'm with him" she said.

"arma" i yelled "what happened?" he came in hurriedly "open the door now" i told him.He ran to the city's Stereoscopic behind me and then i saw nik with her in his hands she was unconscious

"call the doctor now" nik said "what happened to her?" I asked going to him and took her from his hands "gab" he told me. No way. They captured them with gab. "what have he done to her?" i asked him "you know him?" he asked me "answer me" i yelled at him "he beated the hell out of us. Now tell me how you know him!"he said.

I put her on the sofa."Gab is Gabriel. I put him there as a punishment for what he did and to make his mafia weak" i explained. Gabriel was the American mafia boss but when he was their boss the Americans were strong i needed to weaken them. After i put him in abria the Americans got weaken again like they were when they sold my mother.

I heared a knock on the door. "entra" i said (enter). The doctor was in front of me "what happened?" he asked me "she was beaten" nik explained. "you look awful nik" he told him "yeah yeah i know just see what happened to her." nik said and the doctor went to loria to examine her.

"she has nothing broken" he said "just bruises" he continued "so why is she not waking up?" nik asked him "she will" he said and stood up "she will be okay after her bruises heals." he said opening his notes writing down something "just put this cream on her bruises" he said giving me the note "okay" i told him and told nik to go with him outside so he can examine him too

I took her to her room and laid her on the bed she has a bruise on her shoulder other is up her shoulder where i fired the bullet when we were training we didn't get the time to clean or do anything to it.

"kai" she said opening her eyes "I'm here" i told her holding her hand "you okay?" i asked her "where is nik? Is he okay?" she asked ignoring my question and lifting herself up from the bed

"he is okay. He is downstairs with the doctor. Just lay down" i told her "I don't want to. I'm fine" she argued. "okay but bear the consequences" i told her standing up from the bed and was about to open the door and leave when she spoke "don't". "don't what?" i asked her "don't go" she told me "i will see nik and come back" i told her and went outside "nik" i called for him. He was sitting on the sofa in the living room with my mom with checking on him "i want to know why the fuck you went there without telling us? And why you did all of that? You destroyed our project you fool." i yelled at him grabbing him and slamming him into the wall. He whimpered "kai leave him" my mom said "just one minute mother i have to deal with your foolish chid" i told her mentioning her to shut up "answer me goddammit" i said slamming my fist into the wall just behind his face.

"because i wanted to help" he said "help with what? You didn't Want to go there in the first place. Suddenly you wanted to help! And how you damaging our project is exactly help?" i asked him again now seeing Arma and max entering the room

"kai Rilassare" max said. "don't tell me to relax when he put our project in danger."i yelled at max. i hate when people tell me to relax i mean I'm angry as fuck dude when you tell me to relax i won't suddenly relax.

"he didn't just put our project in danger. He put his life and her life" i continued "are you happy now?" i asked him "no kai I'm not. I'm the one that was beaten, I'm the one who was captured and I'm the one who suffered. So don't think that I'm happy that i caused damage to myself along with your project and your girl" he said.

"it is *our project*" i told him "and is she our girl too?" he said earning a punch to his face leading him straight to the floor "Cresci. tu sei nik lionail per l'amor di Dio" i told him (Grow up. you are nik lionail for God sake) "cazzo quel lionail che vuole che siamo perfetti in tutto" he said (fuck that lionail that want us to be prefect in everything) i was about to punch him again for that but i found loria infront of me holding me back

"stop this.. you are brothers for god sake" she said slowly . And I punched the wall instead "this is the second time that i rescue you. The third time i will let you die" she told nik and he smiled

"you are not my children. My children will never do that to each others. Wake up kai not some girl will make you hurt your brother or beat him. I didn't raise you like that" i heared my mon behind me. I don't want to have that conversation right now

"stay where you are and don't you dare take another step" i heared her again forbidding me from leaving

"since you came here there are always problems on my children's head. I want you out from here as fast as possible" my mom told loria. i looked at loria to find her eyes beginning to soften "with all my respect ms lionail but i saved your reckless child twice and.." "because you put it in danger twice" she interrupted her "no his actions are the reasons. He made foolish decisions. Did foolish things. Your lovely boy was in my bed the first time i came here without my acceptance and when i refused he beated me. What raise you are talking about? If you raised him right he won't raise his hands to a woman and your other lovely boy the first time i came here from his fucking project he made his man beat me and was ordered to kill me by the great lionail. With all due respect you are not a family to be so proud of it's name.

Yes you are lionails but you have nothing good to be proud of " she said at my mother's face and went upstairs again.

Her words hurts like hell but she was right we have nothing to be proud of we weren't raised right. Actually we weren't raised at all because my mom was being beaten at that time. I was hurt by her words but i was proud by her standing up to my mother. She didn't let her humiliate her. Questa è la mia ragazza (That's my girl).

"are you happy now? Some little girl made you a fool because you talked without thinking. You are not with us in that world mother. You don't know your children's nature. You are broken and you don't let anyone near you. Don't let anyone tell you that you are wrong. You just want all people to respect you because you are ms lionail" that was max finally out of his silence

"know who you are talking to" my mom warned him "who? My mom. I'm talking to my mom. Wake up mother you have 3 broken children without the ability of love because you just let my father beat you. Beat us all especially kai. Do you know that kai never loved anyone! He don't even know what that means. And that girl you were about to humiliate minutes ago is the only girl that made him have any feelings. Do you know anything about us? You just know the picture of the powerful amazing lionails you know nothing about the Real us." he exploded.

"max.." "don't max me kai she knows nothing. I was 5 years old and have heart problems because of the beating i was having. You know that. You are the one who was making my father turn from me to you. You took all the beating instead.

She knows nothing about that she don't know that we all are afraid to become like them. " he interrupted me

"lei è ancora nostra madre" i said (she is still our mother).

I looked at my broken family they are all broken no one isn't.

"arma take max to the office and gave him his medicine. Nik go to your room and take a shower then come to my office i want you" i gave them orders and they did what i said i was now alone with my mom in the living room

"you didn't raise me mother i raised myself. and my brother too i was the one getting all the beating instead. And that girl is tougher than all the lionails. That girl is the one that i love and i don't like the idea of my girl being humiliating by my mother. So gather your guts and apologize to her because i know that you meant nothing by what you said you were just afraid about your little child" i told her and turned my back to her leaving

"so you want your mother to lose all the respect that she collected all those years by apologizing to some girl!" she said "the respect that you collected with all those beating?" i asked her "yes" i continued and went upstairs to loria's room

"come on in" i heared her voice from behind the door after i knocked on it "loria i want to talk to you" i said entering her room "sure" she said

"look loria i won't talk much. I know nothing about all the love thing and that things but i know that i have feeling for you and i want you to stay with us" i said. Yeah that's it short and clear "i want too kai. But i think your mother have another idea" she said "i don't care" i said before she is able to say another word "take your time to think about it" i said opening the door again to go to my office.

In my office"let's forget all the things that happened in our living room and focus on our work. Arma the city!" i said looking at arma "the city is damaged you need another families to rebuild what the others damaged and you need to get rid of the damaged families" he explained "do it. But leave loria's family" i told him and looked at nik.

"are you going to work with us?" i asked him "in what?" he asked "whatever it is whether it is abria, the mafia or any other work" i told him "yes" he said "you will have to accept that i will be the boss. You will do as i say without questioning" i told him he nodded his head and i looked at max.

"i Want to know what happened those past few days in all the mafias" i told him "the Russians are still searching for a way to get loria. The Americans have made new alliance with the Russians kar is the one leading that alliance. And the Spain mafia wants to do an alliance with you along with the Frances" he said "okay. Tell them that we approve of them joining us and Prepare a meeting soon between us and our alliance" i told him.

"and what will i do?" i heared loria "your work" i told her smirking and she walked towards me "and what is that work!" she asked smiling "my bodyguard" i told her and she smiled "but we will have to get you extra lessons there is no way that I'm accepting you as my bodyguard with you being beaten by gab" i told her smirking. Her smile faded "we will see about That" she told me.

Okay now I'm ready let's see where the days will take us.

Chapter 27

L oria pov

"kai I'm not a child can you make the train harder. Maybe put the target further" i sair smirking and looking at kai's relaxed face.

I was at the field training. I was getting better and better everyday, learning everything that kai knows and that wasn't something easy. Every wrong thing that i did i was getting punished. Not something big though he was just doing small things as punishments like the one time he shot me just above my shoulder the bullet just scratched my shoulder because i underrated him and said that he wasn't going to shoot me. It was somethings to learn from it. Another when i was distracted at the knives throwing so i got a knife inches away from my ear. It scratched me because i moved. that day he didn't work; he was just beside me all day we were having a quite day in the garden.

"i think that you are fully learned now....Except for the fast reflexes" he said surprising me by pulling me into his arms and turning my hand behind my back.

"okay we can work on that" i said. He chucked at me releasing me from his hold and turning me so that I'm now facing him. "yeah i think we can" he said kissing me.

Don't ask me what are we because i have no idea but i really love him so much. I like it when I'm close to him, smelling him, hugging him. I Can't imagine my life without him but I'm worried. I'm worried about lots of things: My mother ;when i left the city i didn't talk to her i didn't understand why she put me there she prisoned me she put me there to be beaten by That punisher man whatever his name was, i was worried about my new powers i now can channel people's minds. Talk to them. Meaning that i can answer kai's thoughts about anything without anyone knowing or listening to what i will say to. him ;arma is helping me with that i don't know how but he knows lots of things about my powers source and how to deal with it.

"what are you thinking about?" i heared kai "mom" i replied. Okay Now he looked stressed what is he hiding? Is he letting his mind open! I tried to see what's on his mind but i found non. He is blocking his mind. Means that he is really hiding something

"what are you hiding ? I asked him still focused on his mind."not hiding. Just not telling you" he said "what is it?"i asked him."if my mind is blocked then i don't want to tell you. It won't change when you ask me."he said his expression now stone cold."okay" i said. What is he hiding from me? i want to know. Is it something about my mom? "is it about my mom?" i channeled his mind "yes" he said loud and clear my heart is now pounding in my chest.

"boss the metting is in 15 minute" i heared someone from behind i didn't move i stilled at me place "Okay" kai said and i heared footsteps behind me getting away.

"come on we are have a metting" kai said getting away from me "i will take a shower and will meet you in the office" i said following him he stopped and looked back at me "the meeting is in 15 minute loria. No time for a bath i think" he said with an cold expression. "okay. A change of clothes then!" i said moving leaving him behind "you are the one wasting the time because of what you are doing right now" i yelled so he can hear me.

"go find loria ORA" i heared kai saying to one of his men outside his office. He waited for me. He didn't go inside without me. "that won't be necessary" i said headed to him. (now)

He looked at me like he is going to shoot me right here... and he is capable of doing it smoothly. I have learned that

I was wearing a dress that he bought with me that day. It was a black tight dress and some black heels. "let's go in shall we?" i asked him standing behind him as his *bodyguard * he opened the office's door and we were met by max's hard expression. It is the first time that i see max with that expression he is usually with the smile expression he is always lovely but not here, not now.

"i don't see a reason for you being late. as i see you are... well; not missing any part." someone said "i don't see that we are late" kai said "what? You want glasses?" the man said to him "actually i want a knife" kai said putting his hands up to me to give him a knife. Also I'm wearing a dress that has no pockets i know that i must have at least one knife. I leaned down pulling the knife out from my thigh belt and giving it to him he took it from me and took the aiming position

"if you move you lose" i told the man "trust me i tried" i continued earning a smirk from kai i know what he is planing

"he won't refuse an alliance like ours" the man said "keep telling yourself that" i whispered and kai aimed and through.

It landed on the man's shoulder "i told you" i said smiling kai looked at the man his face's expression is stone again "i think you should have listened. I was planing on putting it above your shoulder so it will just scratch you but you provoked me" he said going to set in his chair. I went to the man and took the knife out from his shoulder

"you will pay for that. You can say that you now has earned another enemy instead of an alley" the man said putting his hand on his wound "join the club" i joked. "and your bitch as well" he said again standing up from his chair i put my hand on his shoulder putting him down. Kai galred at me "what? You want something little whore?" the man said smirking and i swear to god i saw kai's expression turn to a smirk. I looked at the man "yup actually i want" i said the man's face fall down. He didn't expect me to talk back to him.

I grapped the knife again and put it in his eye earning all the men's attention to me surprised . The man yelled from the pain "oops we need a bandage right here kai" i said faking a sad expression "you stupid whore" the man yelled at me and i smiled taking a step back but the man grapped me choking me but i slamed my fist into his face I was getting better and better at punching and fitness exercises so my punch was strong to make him go to the floor the men didn't move an inch.

"we came here to suggest an alliance kai not to get humiliated" another man said looking at my eyes "and i don't think that you were humiliated. It's just a lesson to not talk like trash to my guard and she is the one teaching that lesson" kai said looking at the man "consider it a warning rugir" kai continued looking at the man at the floor "you can still be our alley if you behaved well".

I walked back to kai and stood beside him "think about it and we will wait for you answer" kai told him "you can go now so you can deal with your *wounds*" he continued

"we can now talk about our alliance" kai said after rugid walked out of the office. I used my powers to see with his eyes i don't think that kai needs me right now.

Rugir walked out from the office looking at the guards his and ours. His guard followed him looking at the floor he is missing an eye and he is their boss after all no one can humiliate him like this.

"call the Russians" he told one of his guards when he got in the car "i can't do that plan..he stapped me for fuck sake.. And his little whore put a knife in my eyes" he was talking on the phone with someone "i will not be your spy i will end him.... What do you mean by i can't?... What?..... I will not go back to him. He humiliated me" he said "loria" i heared kai's voice bringing me back to reality to see that the meeting is still on and everyone was looking at me . I looked at him "yes?" i told kai. He looked at me then said "anyway we will talk again later that's the end of the meeting. Now I have somewhere to be..".

"what did you see?" i heared his mind "later" i used my new power to tell him that so no one can hear us.

"i said no loria" he said stopping suddenly. I pumped into him "but why? You trained me good and i have proven that i can protect myself today and I will not take long also i will be in the house garden not out of the house" i said looking at him

"let her go out man. Loria can protect herself if anything happened" arma said coming from the living room "you are her lawyer?" kai asked looking upset "I'm her friend" arma corrected him "fine go" kai finally said giving up.

I went to the garden after kai told the bodyguards to let me out and i lay down on the grass looking at the sky above me. It looked perfect the sun was beginning to set making the sky kinda orange mixed with blue. It looked so good. I started thinking about my mom. I really want to know what is kai hiding about my mom but he refuses to tell me and he is so flicking good in blocking his mind i don't even know how he does that. But i think it's the benefits of being the smart child in the family.

I was cut by gun shots. I looked at where it came from to find a sniper in a car so far from us but that doesn't stop it from being a dangerous spot to the house. I watched as the men started falling down outside the gate.

i put my hand on my thigh belt grapping a knife and throwing it where the sniper is but before she can hit him. He hit me.But it wasn't a bullet. It was a drug. I tried to channel kai's mind and succeeded "help" is the last thing i remember saying before my vision turn to black.

Chapter 28

Loria pov

I tried to open my eyes but i couldn't. My eyes were so heavy i think it's from the drug

"i think that the boss will make her his special whore" i heard someone talking "that would be a shame if he didn't share with us" another rough voice said. I tried to read their mind to know where they are taking me "she is awake give her another dose" i heard the first man saying and then i felt a syringe getting pressed in my neck

I started to gain conscious but i couldn't open my eyes. I moved my head to the other side because it was aching. Where am i? I asked my self i don't even know who are those guys i tried to open my eyes again and thankfully succeeded

"hello. we met again" rugir said. I looked at him then i tried to channel kai's mind but i couldn't.

A slap was on my face suddenly "what the fuck!!" i said "stop trying to read our minds you stupid witch" he told me slapping me again "we knew about you and if you try to use your tricks against us there will be consequences" he continued "Okay, do you have any other orders?" i asked him "till now no" he replied. Is he really thinks that I'm asking for orders? He didn't get my sarcasm

"dude that was supposed to be a joke. You didn't get my sarcasm" i laughed at him. He kicked me making the chair that i was setting on go to the ground "lock her here till we know what we are going to do with her" rugir told a man standing beside him and left the room.

The man did what he was told to do and went outside after rugir.

I was still on the floor tied to a chair. I started thinking about all the training that i got and non was helpful. Kai taught me to open my hands free by glass and there was non here. Okay loria don't freak out they will get you something to eat of course. They want me alive so they will feed me and i will use anything they bring. Right now I will try to channel kai's mind ;maybe give him any hints to where I'm or he can give me any advice to what i can do

I tried but i couldn't I'm so weak i can't do it i felt some liquid on my mouth. It tastes like iron. Oh great I'm bleeding. That's how they knew that I'm trying to do anything with my powers. But thankfully they don't know about my new powers they just think I'm trying to read there mind okay that's good i will just try to channel kai's mind without them knowing but not now. Now i just want sleep

Kai pov"what the fuck do you mean by you don't know where she is?" i yelled at jan.

Jan is one of my men. He knows everything about the work, loria and the project. He was also supposed to always have an eye on her but she was kidnapped and he was shot but thankfully we got the sniper man thanks to loria's knife. She managed to throw the knife at the sniper man. I think they both fired at the same time and we were trying to get words out from his mouth since then but he refuses to say anything. It's weird though that she didn't use her new powers at all i didn't feel her like that time in abria means that she is not awake yet from that drug. She will sure channel me when she is awake. She is smart and she is trained good. I don't think that she forgot any of her training i made sure of that.

"sorry boss" jan apologized "get the hell out of my sight" i told him and turn my head to focus on the paper work on my desk. "tell them that we refuse" i told arma "but kai.."he started but i interrupted him "no buts arma. We won't allow Them to step on us. They kidnapped her for God sake".

The Russians are asking for alliance. Of all those days they chose now. They are trying to humiliate me by proving that i have lost my mind after she has been taken away from me. That i refused an alliance with the great Russians and that I'm seeking war. And i will give them what they want.

"kai, tell me that you didn't refuse the Russians alliance" mother said entering the office "i did" i said leaving my paper work and looking at her. She is behind furious "have you lost your mind?" she asked me "no mother i haven't but i will soon" i said.

And i wasn't lying i will lose my fucking mind if i didn't get to her, I will lose my mind if i accepted their offer and i will certainly lose my mind if they harmed her.

"don't you think that you are a grown up now?" she asked. Is she really asking ME that question i stood up taking slow steps towards her

"yes mom i think I'm a grown up and not just now. I'm a grown up since the times that i took those beating instead of you,max and nik. I'm a grown up since the years that the doctors were taking so fuckin much time to heal my wounds. I'm a grown up since i helped father in all the mafia's stuff. I'm a grown up since i took the mafia without my willingness because my brothers were acting like fools, like assholes and since you preferred your precious nik after all that " i said. I was taking heavy breathes

"so don't ask me if I'm a grown up or not. Cause you already know the answer to that, don't question my decisions and don't play with me for God's sake" i said now calmly taking my breath and controlling my anger then i went outside. I need a break.

"loria! Loria open your eyes.." i say "it..hurts" she say trying to catch her breath "i know i know but don't close your eyes, please" i begged her "i know that you don't love me.. but.. i want you to know... that... i do" she said closing her eyes

I punched the boxing bag with so much force. That was one of the hundreds scenarios that was on my mind now. I can't let any of them happen to her i need to find her as soon as possible. I went out from the gym "tell arma, max and nik that we have a meeting in 10" i told jan heading to my room to change my clothes.

In 10 i was in my office with arma, max and nik sitting with me discussing loria's problem.

"kai you need to rethink again it's not a small thing. They are the Russians and who even told you that they are the one that took her?" nik said "because of the perfect timing nik. I think you lack some logic" i told him. "okay but what if you are wrong? You will lose a fucking alliance with the Russians" he argued again "since when do you fear the Russians like that?" i asked him leaning back against the chair.

It is really hard to belive that my brother is afraid of the Russians especially nik. Yes he is a playboy, yes he does nothing to help and yes he spends all of his time at the night clubs or with his whores but he never ever fear someone. He has balls.

"I'm not and you know that" he said clenching his jaw "then don't act like it" i told him and turn my head to look at Arma "well arma?" i said waiting for some information that i asked him to collect before "nothing" he said "our only solution is waiting for her to contact any of us" he continued "i will not sit here wait for here to tell me where she is which is something she won't know." "they won't let her see where she is taken to. They won't even let her know if it's day or night. They will just keep here somewhere she can't process where" i continued "so what we are going to do?" max asked "i will tell you exactly what we are gonna do" i said smirking.

Chapter 29

Loria pov

I was still in this cell my back hurts so much. I have lots of bruises everywhere. I don't know where i am neither what time is it. I don't know for how long i will be here

They don't give me enough food or water they just give me what makes me alive they can't risk me dying.

"so are you ready for today's lesson" i heared someone saying while opening the cell.

Yeah and i was getting a new lesson every day and i know that it's a new day by the lessons. Today is lesson 15.

"ready" i managed to say slowly "today's lesson is to lose hope." the man said.

He was a huge man with a serious face

"what kind of tutor are you? Dude your lessons suck" i said "yeah yeah i know but i didn't ask you to love them." he said taking a step forward with the whip with him.

"aren't you bored? Change the punishment dude I'm bored." i said "I'm not" he said and starting whipping me. ....Kai pov

"arma on three" i told arma beside me and started counting.

We started by taking down the snipers by the muted guns then we started shooting the men outside the house.

The house was in a middle of a forest with no one around. We got the location a few days ago after researching and finding lots of houses. Most of the were traps . But finally we got the right house.

"i will go down to the dungeon. Arma come with me. Max and nik get me the boss" i gave instructions and went down to the dungeon.

We started shooting the people down there then we found her cell.

"on three" i mouthed to arma.

The cell was revealed it has an iron door but with a small window up the door so we can see who's in it.

We counted to three then we shot the lock and opened the door. I found Togo In front of me he was whipping her his whip is in his right hand. I shot his hand immediately made the whip fall down and ran to her. Leaving arma to deal with the rest of Togo.

Togo is a deadly assassin his fav torture thing is whipping the people.

"arma i want him alive" i told arma"loria you ok?" i asked her. She looked into my eyes then smiled i put my hand on her waist to help her stand still. She winced but stood up. Taking small steps we got out and i got her into the car.

I texted arma that I'm leaving and that i want the boss along with Togo both alive and breathing.

"loria you ok?" she was setting in the passinger's seat not laying her back on the chair. "mhmm" she responded.

Once we were inside the house i called for the doctor and got her in my room."rest. The doctor will he here in minutes" i reassured her and was going out but she held my hand. "stay with me, please" she whispered "sure" i said and sat beside her

A few days later.

Loria povl was in the gym trying to recover i haven't seen kai since the day he rescued me.*flashback*"stay with me, please" "sure". He was sitting beside me i missed him so much i wish that i can tell him that. i want to ask him a lot of questions. But i don't have any energy so i did something worse.

He was sitting beside me looking at me his eyes are so perfect his smell. I missed his smell even if we are not in a real relationship or even if we have a confusing shitty relationship i still missed him.

His eyes were pouring into mine his cologne is hugging me i want to hug him so much but my wounds won't allow me. I leaned into him while keeping eye contact he stiffens and leaned back but that didn't stop me and I kissed him.*end of flashback *

He stormed out that day from the room and since that day he is refusing to talk to me. I don't see him ever in here. I ask for him a lot but they just refuse to tell me anything.

I finished my training and was going to my room when i heared moaning coming out from his office.

I entered the office suddenly without knocking to find Kai there for the first time seeing him after that kiss. Fucking some girl.

"fuck" i cursed. He turned and looked at me "out NOW" he yelled "no" i said "get dreesed and out please" i told the girl she did what I said "can you get dreesed?" i told kai not looking to him. He got dressed then looked at me

"who gave you the right to dismiss anyone that I'm with?" he said slowly

"where were you?" i asked him looking into his eyes"none of your business" he said."so you were gone for 5 days after i kissed you. Whenever i ask for you they say that you are not there. And you are just busy fucking some whores" i yelled "KEEP YOUR VOICE DOWN" he yelled back.

"why you even got me from them in the first place?" i asked with sad eyes

He started taking slow steps towards me making me take steps back

"that's not your concern. You are my bodyguard. So you are supposed to protect me not me protecting you. I'm sick of your problems" "and I'm sick of you" i interrupted him "I'm sick of your mood swings, from your anger issues, from your enemies, from all your world.. And.. I'm...SICK OF YOU" i yelled

He pushed me towards the wall behind me got my bruised back in touch with the tough wall.

"Ah.." I winced and pushed myself away from the wall earning me to be in his hold. My hand are on his chest with my eyes closed from the pain.

"loria you ok?" he asked me putting his hand on my back "emm" i winced again "get your hands off of me" i told him and opened my eyes with tears in it.

His eyes met mine his eyes now soft, overwhelming, so full with emotions.

"loria I'm sorry. This is why i ran away i keep hurting you. I'm sor.. " he apologized. I shoved his hand away before he can finish his sentence and went to my room walking slowly.

I got in my bathroom stripped from my clothes and went inside the shower. Cold showers is what heals me since my wounds. i feel like my back is on fire. That push was really a reminder for me to remember my grounds. Let him fuck whoever be wants. From now on kai lionail is just your fucking boss. You have to accept it. He has no emotions towards you. Nothing. Just work and focus on trying to get your father.

I turned the water off and went outside wearing an oversized t shirt that reaches my knees with some sneakers and i went downstairs with a stone cold expression that matches his.

"hey loria" arma yelled to me. I stopped and turned to look at him "yes" i responded "you okay?" he asked. I smiled knowing that it's not him who is asking the turned to leave. "where are you going?" he asked "business" I said.

I went to the dungeon opening the cell that has togo in it. He was tied to a chair with his clothes on but was all covered in blood. His blood.

I took the whip and slashed him in his face. He woke up from his sleep.

"hello" i said he looked at me his eyes are furious "what? You are out of lessons?" i asked him smirking. He tried to get up but i kicked him and he went to the ground " i want some information" i said "i will never tell you anything" he responded to me earning me to step on his wounded hand. "you will" i said "when you were whipping me lesson numer 8. You said that if he doesn't want you alive you would have been dead already." i said remembering the pain in That day

That day he was extremely angry. And his whipping were so painful that i was screaming after each whip. That lesson was ths only lesson that mattered to me because i really learned something from it.

"you won't get a word from my mouth" he said "and yes i remember That day. That was ths best day. It was the only day the you were screaming at. I remember that we stitched you that day" he said smirking "you stitched me wrong twise" i remarked while clenching my jaw. "yeah and i had to remove the stitches and do it again and again and again" he said.

I took a knife from my thigh belt and dig it into his thigh but he didn't scream. I want him to scream so hard that my ears will be hurting. I took the knife out and dig it again in another place and again and again till i found someone holding my hand before i dig it one last time.

I looked at the one holding my hand to find that it's kai. He took the knife out of my hand and took me out.

I was breathing heavily from the anger inside me. Kai looked down at me and then he hugged me. I was still for 2 minutes then i pushed him away

"can you keep your distance?" i asked him he looked at me confused

"you okay?" he asked "why i wouldn't be sir?" i said. He raised his eyebrows in surprise "sir?" he asked "yes" i said "you are my boss. What do you expect? " i asked him "I'm not" he said "yes you are" i said "you are fired" he told me smirking. I looked at him with furious in my eyes. "okay" I said

I left him behind and went to the main door but he grapped me stopping me "where do you think you are going?" he asked "out" i said "loria stop it" he said clenching his jaw "what?" i asked coldly. He looked at me then smirked "you asked for it" he said "for wha... " he stopped me by putting his hand on my mouth and pinning me to the wall.

I flinched at my wounds and shot my eyes closed tightly "you keep talking. You don't listen to anything" he said slowly "you are fired from the gurad position. But... You will always be by my side" he continued and moved closer to my ear "Come il mio amante" he said (like my lover).

Chapter 30

K ai's pov
I looked at her waiting for her respond but she didn't she was just staring at me.I raised my eyebrows waiting for answer "so..." i said

"are you seriously asking me that?" she asked laughing. "what do you see?" i asked her clenching my jaw because of her reaction that i don't feel good about.She laughed even more

"you are unbelievable. Tell me kai how many times did you see me since i got back?" she askedAll the time "how many times you asked me how i feel? Do you know if I'm healed or not? Do you know if I'm currently in pain or not?" she asked me every time with different tone 'higher tone'.

I started to get angry at her for raising her voice at me but at the same time i feel sorry that i made her feel this way. But i never stopped checking on her i saw her all the time i was basically stalking her by my cameras.

She pushed me away and took her top off, showing me her full bruised back. "do you know that this hurts as fuck and you just keep pushing me into the goddamn walls. I have had enough kai. I'm getting back to abria" she said her face is red with anger.

I grapped her by her throat and closed the distance between as then i kissed her. I kissed her a tender sweet kiss not some horny kiss. I wanted her to feel what i feel, to know what i wanted to know.

She kissed me back wrapping her hands around my nick deepinng the kiss.

After two minutes i broke the kiss she was breathing heavily. "you are not going back to abria" i said "i am" she said "no you are not" i told her firmly taking few steps away from her "you sill stay her with me" i continued "as what?" she asked.

I looked at myself in the mirror behind her and her bruised back. Her back was now bleeding. "loria stop arguing please" i told her and walked towards her i looked at her back then took her by hands and walked the bathroom.

I went to get the medical bag and when i was back she was holding into the counter closing her eyes

"you okay?" i asked her putting my hand around her waist so that I'm ready if she fainted. "yes" she responded.

I hooked my arms under her and put her on the counter "stay still" i told her she nodded her head. I started cleaning the blood trying not to put her in more pain but failed as she winced once i put the cotton on the wound.

"sorry but there is no easy way" i told her continuing. She grapped the counter and tightened her grip around it "c..can you make it quick" she sluttered. I didn't respond to that. I don't respond on the stupid questions.

After a while i was done i went and stood infront of her. "so about my question?" i asked her. "when you know what a lover is i will accept" she told me. I moved closer to her putting my hands on each side of her waist and my mouth was very close to her ear

"i know what a lover is. May i show you?" i whispered against her ear and planted a kiss on her nick. She shivered. "can you put me down?" she asked me. I released a hot breath against her nick and picked her up to put her down. She was going out from the bathroom.

"where you think you are going?" i asked while holding her by her waist. "kai i want to leave" she said. I turned her and looked at her eyes. I start taking my shirt off

"what are you doing?" she asked her eyes now on the floor with pink cheeks."what do you want me to be doing?" i asked her "n..othing" she said sluttering i chuckled."whatever you want i will do" i told her while putting my hand under her chin making her look at me

She looked at me while her cheeks turning red. I smirked. "you like what you see?" i asked her. She looked away moving her neck so fast that it hurt her. She put her hand on her neck . I looked at her. i know it's nothing it will be over the minute she go out from my office. "karma is a bitch" i smirked.

She looked at me with anger in her eyes but i couldn't help myself she is so fuckin hot when she is mad. I kissed her putting my hands on her waist getting her closer to me. I want to feel her. I want my body to know hers and hers to know mine. She kissed me back with her Pretty lips then she pulled away taking hard breathes.

I took my shirt off and put it on her then i buttoned it and kissed her forehead "I accept your offer" she said.

Chapter 31

I really should stop taking decisions without thinking. I don't know why i accepted his fucking offer but what was i supposed to do if i didn't accept it i will have to go back to abria because I'm really done with him not caring about my feelings.

I was walking to my room with kai's shirt but I'm so unlucky to see arma walking out from the gym with nik and max. Ohh. This is gonna be awful.

"oh look what we got here" arma said smirking. "what?" i asked him playing dumb "i like this shirt where did you get it from?" he asked me still smirking i really want to punch him in his fucking face.

"cut it arma yes this is kai's shirt" i said walking past him he laughed then was about to walk but he was grapped by his neck.

I looked back to find kai still shirtless holding arma by his neck. "kai this position is so sexually uncomfortable" nik said smirking. Arma gulped "if i saw you teasing her again leading her to play any stupid games" he looked at nik then to me. My cheeks heated from embarrassment remembering the kiss between me and nik

"you know what I'm talking about" kai said to arma tightening his hold on his neck "well i will let you wonder what would i do and don't forget that you escaped the last punishment " he continued removing his hand from arma's neck.

Arma started taking long breathes in and out trying to get his breath back to normal.

Kai walked to me putting his hand around my waist and kissed me. The kiss was so good but i really wish that the ground will swallow me now from the embarrassment. He broke the kiss then looked at them

"loria is my lover now" he said smirking "yeah we understood" nik said "then i wish you understand that i don't like her being bothered" he continued then kissed my head and went away.

"you are in a serious trouble little girl" nik said smirking i looked at him and then to Arma "yes she is" arma said Confirming nik's sentence and they started chasing after me. With max still in his place laughing.

I started running from them. I know that they won't do anything harmful but i will not Destroy the game.

I went to the garden out surprised that the guards were not in their position but enjoyed it anyway.

"loria wait" nik said i stopped and looked at him "are you tired already?" i teased him smirking "loria something is odd come back inside" arma said looking around "oh come on arma. This is so easy" i smiled to him.

I was surprised after a few seconds that they were right. Something was really odd. What gave it away? A bullet.

During our chacing game and my teasing to them we found nik on the floor with a bullet in his chest.

I turned fastly trying to see what is happening but i found a black car with some guy out from the window holding a gun into his hands he was aiming now to arma i grapped a knife from my thigh holder i always wear it i never take it off. I grapped the knife and throw it to the man's hand first then i grapped another and throw it to the ties of the car and i didn't mess.

I looked back to check on them then i grapped another knife and throw it into the other tie. And it was easy. Why? Because he was already struggling with his car with one tie has a hole in it. And with the other also having a hole in it the car forcelly went to stop with men coming out from it with guns in their hands.

"take cover" i screamed to arma and took a cover behind a rock.I looked at arma after and found him taking cover behind some wall with nik laying down beside him his shirt is soaked with blood and arma's shirt on his chest keeping pressure on the wound.

I channeled kai's mind (kai we are getting attacked out. Shoot for injury not kill) i told him.

A few minutes passed then we found our men out from the house with the guns and firing around with kai in the front of them it didn't take much time to the fire to stop. They were only a few.

(loria where are you) i heared kai's mind. I stood up and went to where Arma and nik were. "is he okay?" i asked arma "i can't assure you that" arma responded "what happened to him?" kai asked suddenly appearing from behind me with his mind holding so much bad ideas that i couldn't handle.

"get him inside arma" i told arma then went inside. I can't face kai.

I went inside and was met by max "what happened? Are you okay?" he asked "I'm sorry" i said and i went to my room i can't face them. I can't face anyone. I'm the reason behind all these problems. If i didn't come out from this project and has these powers they wouldn't make all these problems to get me.

Kai's povl don't have any idea what the fuck happened but i will know i will know the whole truth from these fucker's mouth i Ordered my men to not kill them all. we shot for injury not kill because we don't have an idea about who they are and what if we didn't kill just one and that one was just a soldier without informations. Something like that never happens without at least one of them knowing what they are doing, the reason for what they are doing or who they are firing at.

I was in my room changing when i heared loria. My first thought was that she is hurt again . She is a trouble magnate. But i was shocked to find nik with bullet in his chest. His wound is heavily dangerous. He is in coma now.

"what the fuck happened Arma?" i asked arma angrily "i don't know. We were just playing around then we found a bullet in nik's chest" arma said "why the fuck you were playing around without your fuckin guns. Since when are you that reckless?" i pushed him to the wall " i didn't think" arma yelled pushing me away. Arma and i are equally strong so when he pushed me i was pushed to the other side of the room.

"that is the problem. Since when you don't think? Since when you go out without your gun?" i asked him with even more anger. These stupid things usually don't come from arma. Neither it happens with nik.."i don't know okay? I was minutes from being killed without saying goodbye kai. When we go to missions i always say goodbye. You know that this is what freaks me the most" arma said.

They were with loria then Loria is the one that will tell me what happened. I went upstairs to her room after asking about where she is.

I opened the door to find her sitting on the bed "loria" i called for her. "yes" she responded without looking at me "what happened?" i asked her. "I'm sorry" she said "about?" i asked her again. She looked at my eyes for only a second then she looked away i would swear that i saw a glimpse of regret. What is she regretting? "I'm the reason behind all these" she continued. "how?" i asked blocking my mind. I can't hurt her with my thinking. "forget it" she said and stood up walking towards the door and past me.

"forget what? Don't skip my questions. How are you the reason to my brother's situation???" i asked her holding her hand to stop her from walking out. "kai let go of me please" she said "no" i replied. In a second she took her hand out and pushed me to the side.

She doesn't want to talk. But why. I have no idea.

In the dungeon"so you were saying that the Russians made you do that and that you were supposed to shoot nik and arma then take loria" i said holding the knife in my hand and slicing his leg open.

He is the only one still alive. Like i thought he is the only one knowing what is going on. He told me everything but i still need to know where are them. This is a war I'm going to attend. No going back or Giving up. They shot my brother. He is in a coma because of them. I have had enough of them

"why don't you try to recall where the main house is?" i told him putting my knife on his chest "or I'm going to put you in a coma just like my brother" i continued."but i don't know where the main house is" he said taking shaky breathes. "maybe when you come back from the coma you will remember" i said pressing the knife further into his chest "stop stop i will tell you" he yelled. "I'm listening" i told him smirking

Back at the office"arma prepare a meeting with all our alliance" i told arma walking out from the office and into nik's room

"I'm sorry ma'am" i heared loria's voice "it's not enough. My son is in coma right now. He is missing his life in this stupid coma. He must be out there enjoying his life not in a bed not able to talk, move or even opening his eyes" my mom was yelling into her face.

"with all due respect ma'am this was his ending he is in a fucking mafia do you think that he was going to die a peaceful death? I'm sorry for your loss, I'm sorry for your pain and I'm sorry that I'm the reason behind THIS situation. But all your kids are going to end like this if they didn't quit this mafia things" i heared loria telling my mother.

"lor is right mom" i said entering the room "and that's why I'm quiting this shit. I will take my brother's revenge then i will take my brothers and my girl and will quit this shitty life. If you want to come with us come. If you don't want to then you will have to live with your traitor husband. Who gave information to the Russians more than once " i told her. "what?" she asked "yes mom your dear husband was the reason behind all these things if it wasn't for him the Russians won't know all these informations about us or our work. And he is taking cover as he is protecting us from loria and making me stronger by putting me in all these problems" i finished.

I looked at loria she was looking at the floor.Loria was the one that told me all these and with investigating i found that she wasn't lying. My father was really leading them to us for an unknown reasons. His reasons were inconvenient so i acted like i never heared them.

"now can you please leave us alone" i told my mom. She walked to nik's bed kissed his forehead then went out

"lor you are not the reason behind these problems. On the opposite you are the solution. If it wasn't for you we would have never knew that my father was selling us to the Russians.." "but if it wasn't for me nik wasn't going to be here now. He wouldn't be in a coma right now missing his life." she interrupted me.

I looked at her and started wondering. Is she right? If she didn't escape abria. Would my brother been here now? Maybe my project wasn't going to fall afterall. Maybe i wouldn't hold my father in the dungeon for selling us to the Russians. Was my father even going to sell us in the first place?

"no, if it wasn't for me nothing of these would have happened" loria said. Shit she heared my thoughts."lor i didn't mean" "i didn't ask" she interrupted me.

I hugged her "I'm so tired. I don't want to be away. I don't want to fight i only have one fight left and it is surely not with you lor" i told her.And it's the truth I'm really tired "i want to fight beside you in that fight" she said hugging me back "no,it's.." "so dangerous yes i know but i won't let you do it alone kai and we will not talk about it. I'm your bodyguard afterall" she interrupted me again pulling away from me "lor" i said taking a step towards her "don't. Ever. Pull away from our hug" i told her then hugged her again.

"so. Will you let me?" she asked me looking up into my eyes "we will talk about this other time" i said.

Chapter 32

Loria's pov

2 months later

"when were you going to tell me?" i asked kai.

I'm so fucking angry with him. He can't control everything like that i won't allow it.

"loria" he began "if you are going to lie then rethink because i already know about what you did and let's not forget my mind reading thing" i warned him.

Few minutes ago"no arma loria will not know about it now." kai yelled at arma. "but she deserves to know" arma explained "not now we have a war coming i can't tell her that now.".

I looked into arma's mind but i didn't catch anything. He was sad about me not knowing about my village. But what happened to it? His mind didn't gave away much.So i looked into kai's hoping that he wasn't blocking his mind because he doesn't know That I'm outside.

I looked into his mind and tried my practice with arma. He taught me that i can see anyone's memories or past thoughts now but i wasn't so good at it i was still a beginner.

I caught glimpses of photos. I think it's memories of him working on his computer, Some working on abria's things and finally i caught some glimpse of him and arma's conversations about abria and kai telling to remove all the data about the people in abria including my own mother and grandma.

I stormed inside his office and started yelling at him.

now"i wasn't going to tell you now loria" kai said sitting on the sofa. "well I'm aware" i said.

"now tell me what the hell is that. I don't understand why would you do this shit." i yelled at him. "loria" arma began but i cut him off. "you shut up arma because you knew about this and you didn't tell me. I thought we were best friends" i blamed him.

But what am i blaming him for? Kai is his best friend and boss. He was surely going to follow his rules and his orders.I don't have any right to blame him.

"so kai! I'm waiting" i told kai turning towards him giving him all my attention.

"loria. There is no time for that. We are in the middle of a goddamn war. You know that. You were the one that told me about the Russians shipment few days ago after you got into that asshole's mind. You were the one beside nik when he got shot. You.." "I'm the reason behind all these" i interrupted him.

"i know that. But i don't deserve to be left in the dark about my own family. My own village. You left me here without any memories. You took their memories kai you can't do that." i told him starting to feel weak.

I have nothing anymore. No family, no memories, i have no home...

"it wasn't supposed to be like this." he yelled slamming his fist on the table in front of him. "i didn't plan to take her memories away. She was the only one that has her memories. But she still didn't get enough. She fought again. Harder. Making more damage in the project. I didn't have a choice" he explained

I looked to his hand now covered in blood. The table was a glass table.

"your project" i said in a sad tone. "you were supposed to end it to leave these people in their lives. We agreed on that kai. We said that we will go away we will leave thia mafia. Will end this project and leave the people to live their lives in abria. They are enjoying their life in there. But you just came in and took all their memories away." i told him.

"they loved each other they didn't want anything else. They were happy with their memories about each other. They have no one. They don't have even have a children you took that away from them. When you made them steriles" i told him.

I knew about this only a few days ago when i was talking to max. He said that they made them all steriles. So they won't experience any pain and because kai have believed that the kids might suffer from their parents like he did. But my parents weren't.

They weren't supposed to enter the village in the first place. But nik put them there. He didn't know anything about the project nor that they made the steriles first. And in the first they weren't in control of the door to the village so they didn't know how to take them out. But kai put some memories into their mind. FAKE MEMORIES. He made mom believe that she has a mother and that my father's mother was died. He made so many things. And when my father began to search he found the door and ran away.

His name was vulian he was one of kai's men but he panished him when he knew that i was out from the project and he didn't get any news about him. He escaped from the exile that he put him in.

Kai was the one who told me about him. And he also told me that he adopted someone when he was here but he didn't tell me whom.

"lor please let it go" kai said taking few steps towards me. I looked into his eyes. I can't forgive him for that. "i will be by yourside in this war. But when we finish.." i stopped and looked into arma who was worried about my next word coming out from my mouth [Η Λόρια δεν το κάνει.] i heared his mind. But i can't. (Loria don't).

"i will leave" i finished my sentence.

Chapter 33

Kai pov

No. She can't go. I won't let her

I didn't argue with her that day but i won't let her go away. And we still have time.

"kai we found their location" arma said opening my office's door. We were searching for the Russians for some time and we couldn't till now

"tell the men to prepare but don't tell them where we are going" i told arma and went out from my office.I went upstairs to loria's room and opened it. To find her changing. She was wearing an oversized t shirt and some ripped jeans. She always look hot in oversize clothes.

"what are you looking at?" she asked. "you" i answered. She looked at me. She is still furious at me for what i did to her family. But i know how to make it up to her. "we have to move prepare yourself" i told her she tucked a gun to her waist. "I'm always prepared" she said smirking.

Loria pov

We were on our way to the Russians. No one knows where we are going except me, kai, arma and max. All the men don't know. Kai made sure that they don't so that no information will leak to the Russians and so the Russians won't know that we are coming. We will have the first kill.

In the battle it's best if you are the first that way your opponent is going to be less confident and you will have the field to your side. And that is kai's technique. Always

We arrived outside the house and the men started shooting. Kai turned to me "don't ever leave my side,Use the knives you are better with them and be careful to dodge" he told me then kissed me.

I grapped my knives and started throwing in a defense way. Meaning that when i see anyone aiming at us i throw it at him to block the kills to be on their side.

Kai started moving closer and closer in each step he takes i recollect my knives from the dead bodies. I always make sure to throw for a kill.

I was recollecting my knife when i felt a sting of pain in my arms i looked at it to see it sliced open. They have a knife thrower. I took cover and channeled kai's mind "be careful they have a knives thrower and he is good" i managed to get into his mind.He looked at me concerned i nodded my head to reassure him that I'm Fine he was taking cover a few steps away from me.

I closed me eyes looking into the men's mind to try to see with their eyes so that i can see where is the knife thrower i kept on moving from one to another and i finally caught him. Or may i say i found her.

She is the one that was after kai when i first came to them i don't remember her name. But i know her. The one kai used me to make her go away. I think she is revenging now.

I took a breath in and got up then throw a knife at her it landed on her shoulder. Kai looked at me in shock. I never miss.I grapped another and throw it but at the same time she was throwing a knife towards me i dodged it and my knife landed on her other shoulder.I don't want to kill her. This will make sure that she is not throwing anything towards us at least for now.

I went to kai he was standing in the open he is so sure that no one is left except the one in the house and the house is surrounded by kai's men. So he is protected now but he didn't see the man throwing a knife towards him from his right. I grapped my gun and killed him instantly but the knife was already on kai's shoulder. I looked at him he was looking at the man.

"merda" he sweared i looked at him not understanding the reason behind his swearing."arma" he yelled "get him a doctor now" he continued referring to the man i shot "what? Is he with us?" i asked "he was" he told me "but he was going to shoot you" i told him not understanding "i surrender" we heared the girl yelling she was grapped by her shoulders that was already wounded by someone i don't know

"finally. Yuriban" kai said smirking "oh how are you old friend?" the guy Yuriban said holding the girl in front of him as a shield "do you think that we are not gonna kill her and you?" kai asked smirking "no. You will but I'm not holding her for that reason. This girl over there. Spared her life so she must mean something that's first. Second when vulian see that I'm holding his daughter he is going to come to defend her and of course me" the guy explained.

Wait a minute vulian? Daughter??

"vulian's daughter?" i asked "yes my dear she is his adoptive daughter" Yuriban said. "and you must be loria. I heared great things about you it's a shame we had to meet like this" he continued

"vulian is dead" arma said coming from behind kai informing kai but i heared him. Kai tensed but smirked towards Yuriban

"your plan won't work because vulian is dead" he informed him.

I looked at kai. How? He said that they know nothing about him. Was he lying??? "you are lying" Yuriban said "ask his daughter she saw him covered in blood minutes ago" kai said looking at the inform of Yuriban. The girl looked at me with furious in her eyes "yes she killed him" she said still looking at me.

"oh dear. You killed your own father?" Yuriban said laughing hysterically. I looked at kai not understanding. Kai looked at the floor.

Shit. The man who was going to shoot kai. I killed him i killed my own father. My eyes widened as i understood what i did. No this can't happen i didn't know him yet.

(Loria don't show him your weakened) i heared kai's mind and i put a fake emotionless face. He is right. I did kill him but i won't let this man get his satisfaction.

"he always wanted to see you. But that's a shame" he said "he alway begged you to let us go" the girl said "yes that's right. He always did. To be honest he always put our plans to kidnape you. We wanted to simply kill you but he said that we kidnap you he wanted to see you. To reunite with you" he explained.

I grapped a knife from my waist and took a step towards him "so you are the reason behind his vanishing" i said "maybe" Yuriban said (loria don't) i heared kai's mind

I took another step towards him "you are going to pay" i told him then i throw my knife at his legs that was appearing from behind the girl.

The girl ran to the other side. I took slow steps towards him. "like my father begged you to let us reunite. I will make you beg for mercy" i told him then i took my special knife and dug it into his knee.

Chapter 34

Loria pov

"lor please speak to me" kai said from behind my room's door.

He is so capable of just breaking the door and going in but he chooses to talk me into opening it for him. He don't want violet. Yet

"just go away kai, really. I'm not ready for this talk yet" i said.

He is trying to talk to me since we got yuriban. But i refuse to even look at him. For many reasons. He knew that the man i shot was my father but he didn't say anything. Okay it wasn't the time but don't use his death to advantage you. To tell yuriban to surrender because vulian is already dead and That he can't help him.He didn't just avoided telling me the truth but he enjoyed it.

I killed my father because i was defending him that's what i get from this world.

"Loria i know that you are hurt but don't be all by yourself. It won't make it easier. Just open the door so we can talk" he continued."no" i said and went to the bathroom.

Let him say whatever he wants i want to have a shower right now. I took my clothes off and opened the water. Standing underneath the shower head i closed my eyes and enjoyed the cold water running all over my body. I really like these cold showers.

"you should have opened the door when i asked politely" kai said.

I turn fastly to see him standing beside the door leaning his back towards it, looking at me. I quickly grapped the towel and put it around myself.

"really?" he said smirking. I went past him leaving the water still running in the bathroom and walked into the dressing. I took a hoodie and put it on then went back to my room and sat on the bed. He went to me crouching in front of me. I looked at him. I really want to smack his fuckin face right now.

"what?" i asked him "look Loria, okay i get it that you are mad. You have every right to be right now. But can we re-think again! How was i supposed to tell you that it was your father?" he asked me"look kai i don't give a shit about that. All i care about is that I killed my father. And not just that i put nik into coma, my mother and my whole village don't have any memory of me anymore and it's all because of this fuckin world and this goddamn project of yours. So forgive me but now you not telling me that it was my father is my least problems" i snapped at him.

"lor nik isn't in this position because of you. Neither is abria's problem. These are MY effects. from MY doing. So stop blaming yourself okay?" he said with so calmness in his voice that i wish that i had.

"look kai this war is over now. We got yuriban, your project is good, everything is going well. Now i want you to get me back into abria" i told him

"what?" he said standing up "you heared me" i told him my eyes are still where his eyes were. "what do you mean Loria? You want to go back to abria? Didn't you tell me that you don't want to go there again and that you are finally out of it?" he asked me. "yeah. But my village is peaceful. When I'm there I'm safe." i told him. He looked at the floor. "okay" he said and went out.

I'm ready to go home.

Kai pov "bring me arma and max" i said to one of my men

I can't make her stay with me by force i will do what she wants.

"you asked for me kai! " arma said entering the office "yes arma come on in" i said "what do you want me for?" he asked "you will know when max come" i replied and started working on my computer to prepare for sending loria back.

"yes brother" max said entering the office. "since you are here max i can say what i want you guys for" i began "loria is leaving back to abria i need you to get a power source and prepare some memories to put into the people's mind" i finished.

"wait. What?" max said "what you heared max and there in nothing to talk about" i told max.

Arma looked at me confused not understanding. But he won't discuss it now i know that. Arma never talk back to me especially not infront of anyone. He knows that this makes me angry.

"just tell me why" max said. "get a source of power max and you Arma will do the memories part" i said and started working again on the computer.

A few hours later

"are you sure?" i asked her. She was in my office now after preparing everything and getting the power source to provide the city's door. Arma tried getting some memories but he failed. Somethings can't be solved. Epically not getting back something that was hard to collect in the first place.

She looked at me then to max and arma. "I am" she said. "you have 10 minutes to say your goodbyes" i said giving her my back

I heared her moving but didn't hear her saying anything nor could i feel where she moved to. Then i heared the office's door being closed. I turned to find her standing behind me arma and max weren't in the office anymore.Stupid fucking men.

"they aren't" she told me smiling.Get the hell out of my mind loria. "you are the one not blocking your mind anymore" she said still smiling "there is no need to. You will not be here anymore so no one is going to read my mind." i said "yeah" she said her smile fading

I moved to the computer but she grapped my hand and turned me towards her.

"i.." she started but i shut her down by kissing her. She kissed me back. Her lips are so soft and nice I'm going to miss these lips.

She broke the kiss and took a step back taking her breath. I glared at her and grapped her hand making her smash against my chest

"i told you before to never break a kiss" i said smirking.

She smiled and hugged me. I'm not a hugger I'm never really comfortable in hugs. But her. She is never not comfortable. I'm enjoying her hug.

"you have to go" i said leaving her warm arms surrounding myself by the coldness again.

She looked at me and nodded.I opened the door to abria and looked at her she took a step towards the door and looked at me "i will wait for you" she said her eyes watering "at the spot we chose" she continued.

"i.." i started but before i can continue she took the last step and went to the other side of the door.

Chapter 35

Loria's POV

My roof has always been an escape place . escape from reality ,from fighting and even from responsibilities when I was a kid .I have always escaped responsibilities. Was even a lazy kid. How am I supposed to be responsible now! Without my mother ,Without grams . Without anyone I'm alone in here. After kai deleted all my memories in people's head .my own mother didn't know me . Of course they failed to take it back but they succeeded in putting new player in their game. They put me here with a fake name. All the people in abria knows me as kaila. The library owner. Well at least they put me in a place that I used to love . I live here too . Thanks to arma he made the library's roof like a house to me. With the sky showing. He made the room's roof with glass so that I can always look at the sky even if I know that it's not real sky. They made such a great job in editing the sky so that no one else knows that it's fake.

I get to see my mom. Of course she doesn't know that I'm her daughter but better than nothing I guess. She comes to the library everyday I don't know since when does she likes reading but I'm glad that she does anyway.

"Hello Ms Jones. How can I help you?" I asked the entering lady . "I want a history book .what do you suggest to me !"she told me "what century do you want the book to talk about?" I asked her again "I don't know I'm new at readings history books . You choose " she said "okay . Have a seat and I will be back in a minute " I told her.

A normal day in library. People don't know what they want . They just want something to keep them busy. To work their mind a little . But not a specific thing . Even my mom . She comes here daily reading in the library . She reads books that I'm surprised that she understands.

I still have. My powers but I stopped using many of them. I stopped using the chaneling part . I still read people's mind and sometimes I use the other one. But only in specific times.

"Here is your book ms Jones " I handed her the book "thank you" she said and went out . That was the last person inside before I close the library and going up to my roof .

The sky is cloudy but I do like the clouds so I'm not upset . Laying down on my bed looking at the clouds imagining the faces of the people i once loved and the people i still do love

.

I wonder what kai is doing right now. I know that i can use my powers but what is the point he won't respond to me he will just feel me. Feel my presence but he will choose not to respond he would rather feel my presence but never making me feel his.

In the little time that we had together i recognized that he is not the man that i wanted. Not my prince charming. But he was definitely the one i loved. I don't know why or when. Or why do i get jealous thinking that he will move on. The thought of him with someone else. It kills me. And thought that he didn't tell me to stay also kills me. Did he want me gone so he can have someone else?Maybe he didn't want to be the villain but he liked that i was the one who took the decision. So many thoughts that are not important. You need to focus on yourself loria. Just YOU.

Next day. "yes it definitely is one of the most popular books that we have in this section and it's brilliant" i told ms via while taking six of crows book from the shelves and handing it to her. "thanks dear for your recommendation" she thanked me and then she went out.

Well she was the last customer and with that we close and go to the roof. My favorite part.

No please not another customer. sometimes i wish that we didn't have this bell.

"sorry but we closed for today. you can come back tomorrow morning" i said my back facing them.

" oh i won't bother you i already found what i want"

a voice coming from the door said. a voice that i know so well. A voice that made me this.

*please tell me that you are in your office working with arma * i channeled kai. "actually in a library talking to a beautiful girl with shoulder length hair and she is not responding to me" he said

I turned around to see him looking at me with his hands in his pockets. He looks the same. He didn't change not even a bit. He was wearing a black trousers and a white shirt with the the first buttons opened looking at me with a look that i never saw in his eyes.

"i know that we agreed to meet in a different place but you didn't show up" he said smiling

"i.." he interrupted me with a kiss that i was searching for everyday since that night.

Epilogue

L oria pov.

"no kai you put this in the fictional section" i told kai who was about to put six of crows at the history section."how do you manage to know all these?" he asked me."it's not hard baby. You just have to focus on the books in your hands" i told him giving him another book to put it back to it's place on the highest shelf.

He went up the stairs and put it where its supposed to be and went down.

"i really want Arma to see you with these books all around you and you can't decide where to put them" i laughed. And then remembered arma. He was my friend too. I really miss him.

"you really couldn't leave the door so we can see them! " i told him."yes. It would have put you and all people here in risk. And what do you want from them you have the channeling power you can contact them anytime." he told me his hands around my belly."but i really wanted them to be with us." i said my eyes starting to water. He rolled his eyes. "Your hormones are really hard to deal with lor" he told me.

"but i really wanted to see them you didn't have the right to do this" i told him "what do you want to do with them? they are good lor. Nik is leading the business, max did lots of projects and arma finally found the partner he wanted. Aren't you happy for them?" he asked me

"i do. But i really miss them" I used my puppy eyes and looked at him. "alright" he huffed and then used his power.

Yes he got a power because he did exactly what i did. He broke the door to abria so he gained a power

"heyyyy" i shouted. Arma and erini looked at us "hey loria. Wow your buddy got bigger" arma told me mentioning my belly. "yes he did and he will be with us any minute now" i told him. "you listen to me if he is a boy you will call him arma" arma told me.

"wait wait she will call him max" max said coming to screen behind arma. " no she won't" arma argued . "or maybe she will be a girl and they will call her erini". Erini said getting behind Arma. "guys guys" i tried to call for them.

Ouch. What is this..

Kai pov

They will never grow up. They are fighting over our baby's name like we will listen to any of them.

"you okay lor?" arma's question got me from the world that i was in.

I looked at loria she was holding her belly with her eyes closed. " lor" i called her.She didn't respond."lor" i said turning to her closing the image of max and Arma that i once opened so she can contact them.

"lor you okay?" i asked her putting my hand on her back. She looked at me her eyes watering. "i think the baby is coming" she managed to say between tears.

I carried her bridal style and went straight to her grams. She is the one who delivers all babys here since there is no hospital.

"ahh kai hurry up" loria shouted putting pressure on her belly "okay okay you will be okay lor just take a deep breath." i told her running.

"grams help me" loria said once she saw her Grandma.." she is in labor" i told her.

Loria used to call her grams after the memories faded from their head she told her that she remind her of her grandma and she accepted it.

"okay okay darling just push when i tell you" she told her .Loria looked at me and held my hand tight. "I'm afraid" she told me. "don't be. You will be alright. We will go out with our baby. And we will be the happiest family in abria" i told her kissing her head.

"Alright push" her grams told her.She did and screamed putting pressure on my hand and putting her head in my neck."again darling one last time." her grams said again. She did and we heared little scream that made my eyes water.

"he is a boy" her grams said. She looked at me with tired look. I smiled and kissed her. She kissed me back her hand on my chest."he is beautiful" i told her when i carried him into my arms. She tried getting up and i helped her putting my arm on her lower back supporting her. She looked at the baby and kissed him.

"hello little nirax" she said. I looked at her confused "nirax?" i asked " nik. Arma and max" she said smiling.

I kissed her again smiling into the kiss. I really never thought i would be that happy.